Novels by Annabelle Lewis

The Carrows Family Chronicles

Charlotte McGee, Book 1
Titan Takedown, Book 2
Carrows Justice, Book 3
The Bad Penny, Book 4
Fisher of Men, Book 5

Short Story

Caliburnus

Mr. Hyde

BOOK 6
THE
Carrows Family
CHRONICLES

ANNABELLE LEWIS

Publisher's Note

No part of this book may be reproduced, scanned, or distributed in any printed or electronic form without express written permission from the publisher. The scanning, uploading, and distribution of this book via the Internet or any other means without the permission of the publisher is illegal and punishable by law. Please do not participate in or encourage piracy of copyrighted materials in violation of the author's rights. Purchase only authorized editions.

This book is a work of fiction. People, characters, places, events, and situations are the product of the author's imagination. Some historical names, celebrity names, and actual venues appear in the novel in order to place the story in a historic or modern cultural perspective, but these names are used in an imaginary context and do not suggest that any of the incidents ever happened, or the celebrities endorse the work, or participated in any way.

Contact Annabelle at annabellelewisauthor@gmail.com

Text Copyright ©2020 Annabelle Lewis
All rights reserved.
ISBN-13: 978-1-7343757-2-5
ISBN-13 ebook: 978-1-7343757-3-2
First Edition
Publisher: PePe Press
Cover Design: JD&L Design LLC
Editing: Jill Welsh; jwelsheditorial.com
Interior Design: Manon Lavoie

For the Rebel Alliance, you're one with my heart.
An otherwise focused shout-out to you know who...
Two words. One finger.

The Carrows Family Chronicles

Carrows Family

Henry Carrows - Patriarch, head of the clan. Henry's father was Hank.

Julia Carrows - Family matriarch.

Charles Carrows - Oldest child. Charles has hotels/casinos in Atlantic City, Las Vegas, and London.

Angelica Renner Carrows - Newly married to Charles. Pregnant in Book 5, *Fisher of Men*, with twins.

Charlotte Carrows Macchi - Middle child. As a young girl she changed her name to Charlotte McGee, but then changed it back to Charlotte Sofia Carrows. After her marriage to Alex Macchi, she became Charlotte Sofia Carrows Macchi. Mother of Petunia and Lily.

Carey Carrows - Youngest child. Often works for Charles. A free spirit, flirt, and party girl. Often prickly and difficult to control.

Petunia Carrows Macchi - Charlotte's child with David Torres Cordoza. Born in Book 1, *Charlotte McGee*. Adopted by Alex Macchi in Book 3, *Carrows Justice*.

Lily Carrows - Charlotte's child with Alex Macchi. Born in Book 3, *Carrows Justice*.

Whispering Cliffs - The ancestral family home in California.

Macchi Family

Anthony Macchi, Sr. - Patriarch. Deceased in Book 2, *Titan Takedown*.

Marie Macchi - Matriarch. Lives in Bay Ridge, NY (Brooklyn).

Alex Macchi - Private investigator hired by Julia in Book 1, *Charlotte McGee*. Married Charlotte Carrows in Book 2, *Titan Takedown*. Adopted Petunia Carrows in Book 3, *Carrows Justice*. Father of Lily with Charlotte.

Tony Macchi - Cop in 10th Precinct, NYC. Married to Abby. They have a boy named Riley.

Michael Macchi - Alex's partner in Macchi & Macchi. Married to Lauren. Michael and Lauren have two children, Leonor and Andria. The girls are cousins and good friends of Petunia Carrows Macchi.

Nick Macchi - Youngest boy. Lawyer. Runs Macchi & Macchi, London.

Isabella Macchi Laferty - Youngest and only daughter of the Macchi family. A good friend of Charlotte's. Isabella is a schoolteacher and married to Finn Laferty.

Finn Laferty - married to Isabella. Owns a farm outside Ithaca, NY. Prominently featured Book 2, *Titan Takedown*.

Renner Family

Angelica Renner Carrows - Charles Carrows' wife. She enters the series in Book 3, *Carrows Justice*, and uses an alias of Daizy Durand.

Dr. Patrick Renner - Angelica's father. Surgeon. The family lives in San Antonio, TX.

Natalie Renner - Angelica's mother.

Hailey and Diana Renner - Angelica's siblings.

Macchi & Macchi

Family-owned security and private investigations firm. The Carrows' go-to for all matters regarding personal security, hotel and casino security, muscle, and investigations—clandestine or otherwise. Branches in Manhattan, Los Angeles, and London. Anthony Macchi, Sr. began this firm, but passed away in Book 2, *Titan Takedown*. Oldest son, Alex, along with his brother Michael, now run it. Nick Macchi, the youngest, came on board in Book 4, *The Bad Penny* and now runs the London Branch.

Renzo Castrogiovanni - Bodyguard for Charlotte and her family. Single. Divorced.

Luco - Bodyguard for Charles and his family. Brooklyn-born friend of the Macchi family. Served in the military.

Sean Murray - Brother of Connor. Brought in for dirty deeds.

Connor Murray - Brother of Sean. Brought in for dirty deeds.

Santiago (Santa) - Brought in for dirty deeds.

Baach, McKenzie & Blake

Legal firm used by the Carrows with branches in LA, NYC, and London.

Oliver Baach - Founding partner of Baach, McKenzie & Blake. Close personal friend of the entire Carrows family.

Bruce McKenzie - Firm partner.

Allen Blake - Firm partner, criminal law specialty.

Recurring Characters

Bacon - The Carrows family's go-to hacker.

David Torres Cordoza - Petunia Carrows Macchi's biological father.

John and Rosita Gonzales - Factotum/staff at Whispering Cliffs. Have lived on the property since the Carrows children were young.

Harley - Carey Carrows' sometime paramour.

Cheryl Davis - Cherrie Corona - Paula Butler - Geneva Crawford - Friend of the Carrows family. Go-to for help on sting operations. She was born Cheryl Davis. Her stripper name was "Cherrie Corona" at an LA bar named Lacey's. Paula Butler was her alias used in Book 3, *Carrows Justice*. Geneva Crawford was the alias she used in Book 4, *The Bad Penny*. In Book 5, *Fisher of Men*, she returns with her birthname, Cheryl Davis, and is the manager of Angelos, a successful nightclub in Carrows London.

Jaqueline Dunn - Charles Carrows' primary personal assistant.

Tabitha Chapman - Henry Carrows' personal assistant.

Lloyd Greiner - IRS agent in Book 2, *Titan Takedown*. The family worked with him on a sting operation in Atlantic City.

Brandon Linnington - Son of Barford and Jane Linnington, Earl and Countess of Hambley. Brandon is an attorney in London who met Cheryl Davis in Book 4, *The Bad Penny*.

Linnington jewels - Reference to a parure of jewels originally owned by the Linnington family in Book 4, *The Bad Penny*.

Marcel Broussard - A personal friend of the Carrows family and go-to for sting operations. Based out of New Orleans and introduced in Book 4, *The Bad Penny*. He owns the Broussard Gallery and has a dog named Steve.

Alana Whittaker - Head of Carrows public relations.

Summer Ash - Head of Carrows public relations in London.

Sir Hugh Brocklesby - New Scotland Yard investigator. Knighted by Queen Elizabeth for personal service.

JULY

Chapter 1

Freya Brown, a student at St. Petersburg State University in Russia, slowly walked down University Embankment by the River Neva, which flows into the Gulf of Finland and then the Baltic Sea. In a fog, she was thinking about her purpose in life as she returned to her dormitory from an unsuccessful yet eventful trip to the Bakery Madeline far off campus.

Freya was taking a summer semester to study abroad in the beautiful city founded by Peter the Great, but she was actually a student at the University of Edinburgh in Scotland. Along with another girl from Scotland, Mary, they'd moved to St. Petersburg at the end of May. Now, eight weeks into the course, and sweltering in the July heat, Freya was lonely and missed her school in Edinburgh and her family and friends in Scotland. Hoping to raise her spirits, she'd, unsuccessfully, tried to convince Mary to venture off campus with her to the new Bakery Madeline, which was a familiar restaurant chain from their homeland.

"I promised me parents I'd make the most of this adventure, Mary. So with ye or not, off I go," informed Freya.

Hoping that a bowl of her favorite soup would bring her some comfort, instead she had another odd encounter with the Russian culture and an inner conflict between some new strength that was growing inside her and the young girl whose only desire was to crawl back home and forget about conquering the world.

Since its recent opening, Bakery Madeline had been wildly popular and Freya arrived unprepared for the scene. She found herself in a press of bodies, everyone eager to enter. Enduring a long, hot wait, she eventually made it to the front—only to be confronted by a manager, who, on some sudden whim, perhaps hoping to disassemble the crowd, announced there would be a minimum order of 3,000 rubles. Three thousand rubles—or roughly €43—was much more than Freya wanted to spend, even if it meant sacrificing her plan to enjoy a delicious bowl of soup. But Freya, or rather the *inner* Freya who sometimes surprised and continually challenged the shyer girl within, decided to make a small scene over the injustice of this decision for the people who could not afford it.

Her heart beat rapidly as she stared boldly at the restaurant manager making the announcement and yelled, "This is not right! I've been waiting two hours in the hot sun to enter and walked for miles to reach you. This lass here," she'd said, pointing to a young waitress who was red-faced and sweating, "has been thoughtful and offered us water, but *you* just see us as cattle? You could have posted a sign about the minimum purchase when you opened this morning, so those who can't afford your prices wouldn't have waited! Let the people who have been waiting have a chance to order whatever they can afford!"

The manager had other thoughts and asked her to leave. Freya, startled by her outburst, realized it was time to go. Her eyes connected with the young waitress who had been kind to them. She raised a hand in her direction, mouthed the words, "Thank you." Placing her hand over her heart, she smiled as she left.

Dejected by the fact she'd gotten no soup, she was energized by the thoughtful waitress. She'd been kind and Freya connected with her, albeit briefly. What also interested Freya was the supposed randomness of how certain people were thrown into one another's paths. People affected each other in ways that could be unexpected, complex, and unknown. She'd been touched by the young waitress and some of the other patrons who'd supported her efforts. Hope and courage were sometimes elusive in her loneliness, but she'd found them again in an un-expected place.

Smiling at the thought of stopping at the market for some crisps and fizzy water for herself and Mary, she quickly walked past a string of abandoned buildings. Her heart lurched when two men jumped out of a doorway and violently pushed her inside. She struggled to scream, but they held something toxic and strong over her mouth and nose.

Her world went dark.

MARCH

FIVE MONTHS EARLIER

Chapter 2

GENERAL CONTRACTOR CHRIS RICHARDSON did not like disappointing his clients. It was particularly upsetting to let down his favorites. Two of which—Charlotte Carrows Macchi and her husband, Alex—stood near him in the demolished kitchen of their home in the West Village.

"I appreciate the problems you're having, Chris," Charlotte said, "but you promised we would be able to move back in no later than Labor Day, and now you're telling us Christmas?"

Chris gazed into the captivating green eyes of his beautiful client and swallowed hard as Alex frowned at him. "Look, guys, I'd do almost anything for you. You've got to know how much I respect you both, and working with you on this project has been a highlight. Truly. I'm trying to keep things moving along here, but I've been torn over the problems some of my subcontractors are having. I'm trying to help them stay in business and keep my clients happy at the same time. I'm juggling everything the best that I can."

Chris wasn't kidding when he said he liked Charlotte and Alex. When they'd initially met, he hadn't known what to expect from one of the richest and most famous families in the country. As a general contractor in New York City, he'd met a wide swath of the rich.

What he'd found, however, was a couple who were, surprisingly, down-to-earth. They commanded respect, but they also shared that respect with everyone around them. Their West Village project of combining two townhomes into one was a fantasy job, which he was certain would become the centerpiece of his portfolio. The Macchis had the budget to make their residence into one of the most luxuriously tasteful homes in the city, and from the beginning, it had been a dream job with a dream client. Working through the issues that, inevitably, arose with the architects, designers, and contractors during any construction project could be emotionally challenging, especially if the client became unreasonably demanding. His job was to coordinate the team and keep them on budget and on schedule. He was loathe to let Charlotte and Alex down by giving them the bad news.

Alex exhaled. "What exactly is the problem with the subcontractors? We chose you based on your spotless reputation, and you promised that our project would be your top priority, so I'm a little unclear about what the real issue is here."

Chris nodded. "I appreciate your regard for my reputetion, and I want to live up to it. Look, normally I don't like to gossip because I think—especially in my industry in this city—it's a small world. I don't typically take sides and get involved because unless you've 'lived' the project, you rarely get the real story from anyone. That said, I've been trying to help some of the subcontractors who are in a bind because they got screwed over by Hyde Sutton on the work they did for him at Sutton Tower."

Everyone in the city was familiar with the name and reputation of Hyde Sutton, and most seemed to have a legendary story about their association with him. Chris was no exception, and despite his typical position as Switzerland, this time, he couldn't stop himself from getting involved.

"What happened at the Tower?" asked Alex.

"From what I've been told, Hyde had a superheavy hand in all the decisions and created a lot of headaches with multiple change orders; it was chaos. He had teams of subs working around the clock to get that place done. Hyde was making promises, keeping everyone jumping, and pressuring them to pull off their other jobs. Then, when the project was complete, he said he wouldn't pay them because he didn't like their work. He had cabinet makers, painters, interior decorators, glass guys, plumbers, and electricians—everybody who worked on Sutton Tower got screwed. I mean, the man brought in a lawyer and called the subs in one at a time to just flat out tell them he wouldn't honor their contracts."

Chris ticked off the points with his fingers. "Supposedly, because he had already paid enough; he didn't like their work; or the change orders were incorrect, and the overages and overtime weren't his problem. Even though he'd created the chaos, in the end, Hyde and his lawyer just crushed everyone."

Chris shook his head in exasperation. "Some of these guys had been working for him exclusively for like six months. And they're small, you know. Some of them—most of them really—are family-owned businesses, and they had to pay *their* bills. The subs paid for their supplies and labor upfront, and now many are facing bankruptcy. They'll lose everything because the money they thought was coming to them isn't."

"How can he get away with that?" Charlotte's brows knit in confusion.

Chris shrugged and threw up his hand. "He just can! He can, and he did. He told them they could try to collect, but that if they did, they'd better lawyer up—very threatening. He told them that he was a successful businessman because he wasn't afraid to use anything in his arsenal to overpower his opponents. He uses his attorneys to delay judgments and break companies rather than pay them. The strategy apparently works for him because he keeps using it over and over. He has enough money in the bank to outlast his smaller and under-resourced opponents. Some give up, settle for less, or go bankrupt. The ones who settle and take the so-called 'deal' have to sign confidentiality agreements, but I hear they're taking dimes on the dollar rather than lose it all."

"And some of them are working here on our project?" Charlotte asked.

"Yes, a few of them, actually, which is the problem. I shouldn't tell you this, but I've taken a risk hiring a couple of them rather than working with my usual guys because I felt bad for them. I know how hard it is to keep the doors open, so I offered to float them; I paid some of them upfront and gave them time to work extra jobs to rebuild their bank and their book of work. I'm afraid that's the reason that we're running so far behind schedule.

"I'm sorry, guys. It was my call, but I have to tell you that I'd do it again, even though it might hurt our relationship. I'm hoping that's not the case, and, believe me, I'm not just trying to take advantage of your good natures... it's just that

I feel like I needed to help on this one. These guys have families to support, and some of them are really close to the edge now that they lost six months of income for six months of work."

Charlotte shook her head. "I've heard about the games some contractors play with their customers with delays and upcharges, but I've also met Hyde Sutton, so I believe you. How many contractors do you think Hyde played this game with?"

"I'm not sure, but at Sutton Tower, he messed with all of them. I think everyone has heard the rumors about him and his 'ethics,' but he's such a good liar that people believe he won't do it to them, just because he gives them his word. But, of course, his word is meaningless."

Alex frowned. "And you say some of these subs are working on our project? Which ones?"

"The cabinet maker, carpenter, and electrician. That's really all I could afford to take a risk on, and I'm sorry again that it's causing delays. I have complete confidence that they'll finish the job, but they're really stretched for time. I accept the responsibility."

Alex, his mouth in a hard line, turned to Charlotte, as Chris held his breath, wondering what they'd do. Charlotte raised her brows at him, a side of her mouth turning up and then nodded.

Alex returned his wife's smile, then gave Chris a level stare. "I tell you what, I'd like to talk to these subs about the position they've been placed in. If it's okay with you, I'd like our attorneys to join the meeting, as well."

Chris opened his eyes wide with alarm.

Alex put up his hand. "Not to give them a hard time, Chris. Understand, we'd like to help them. Maybe Baach,

McKenzie & Blake will shake loose some cash from Mr. Hyde and give these guys some relief. If their stories are supportable, we want to help. They shouldn't be ruined just because Hyde's got an attorney and the staying power to crush them."

Charlotte smiled at Alex and reached out to hold his hand. Chris hadn't known exactly what to expect from his clients that morning, but he certainly hadn't expected this. Humbled by their patience and generous offer of aid, and their support of his own decision to help the subs, made him emotional.

Before he could react, Alex said, "As a matter of fact, Chris, go ahead and put the word out that we'd be willing to take a meeting from *any* of the contractors who were hurt at the Towers by Hyde Sutton. Give them my number. We'll vet them, and if they got screwed by this guy, we'll see what we can do to help. You have my word, and that actually means something to me."

Chris ran a hand down the side of his face and shook his head. "May I ask why you're willing to do this?"

Alex turned and winked at his smiling wife. "Because, as you said earlier, it's the right thing to do. And I'm a Carrows—only by marriage, mind you—but I've learned a thing or two about not turning away when you might be able to help. We do what we can, when we can. So let's see what we can do for these guys. From what I've heard and seen, Mr. *Hyde* has no moral compass, so let's point him in the right direction. He's a big bully who's picking on the little guys. Let's see how well he does when he comes up against us and Baach, McKenzie & Blake."

MAY

Chapter 3

HYDE SUTTON WALKED through the massive baroque-style living room of his newly completed penthouse at Sutton Tower. Greek-inspired, gold columns lined the room under a ceiling layered with recessed gold and elaborate murals around huge crystal chandeliers. Gleaming white marble floors and white sofas alongside French chairs and furniture were scattered throughout. Hyde ran a finger along the side of a gilt mirror on the wall as he made his way into the kitchen where his wife, Pravdina, and their eleven-year-old daughter, Simone, were having breakfast. Inspecting his troops, he kissed his daughter on the head and gestured for her to rise. "Okay, let me see you. Stand up and give me a twirl."

At his command, Simone jumped out of her chair with a wide smile and complied. This being a Saturday, she wasn't in her sixth-grade school uniform but got to choose—to an extent—what to wear. That morning, she and her mother had chosen a tweed, multi-yarn jacket from Juicy Couture over a graphic T-shirt and short skirt. His daughter also wore leggings under her Gucci leather knee boots, and her hair was pulled back by a jeweled headband.

Simone Sutton twirled around. Nodding at his daughter, his eyes glowing, he felt supreme gratification that she was always so anxious to please him. He knew that each day she looked forward to his approval. Reinforcing her confidence and his belief that she was the most beautiful girl in the world, he let the compliments flow.

"Just look at you. So beautiful! But isn't it a little downmarket for the city?" Hyde Sutton pursed his lips, uncertain.

"Dad! I've got my leotard on underneath! I have dance!"

"Oh, I know, I know." He held up his hands to stop the avalanche of explanations. "I just want you to remember that when you leave this home, and my building, you're representing my brand. We have to be our best and look our best because we're Suttons! We're not regular people."

He turned his attention to his wife. Thirty years younger and practically purchased off a Paris runway, he had high expectations for her in every department. "Pravdina, what do you have on over there. Your turn." Hyde twirled his index finger at her face.

Thirty-five-year old Pravdina closed her eyes and sighed. She looked wearily at him, but stood, revealing a casual purple boucle, cowl-neck sweater dress worn slouchy off of her slender shoulders.

Hyde walked closer to her and said, "Okay, now do a spin for me."

Doing as instructed she cringed slightly when he slapped her ass. He laughed loudly. "Yeah, now there's what I like to see! Looking good, Prav!"

Tiring of his girls, Hyde turned his attention to the room and spotted his twenty-five-year-old French cook, complete with the papers to prove it. Enjoying how she filled out the French maid's uniform, Bijoux had originally been hired from France as an au pair. Hyde chose the country of import based on his desire for Simone to be fluent in a cultured language other than English. Simone would learn nothing but bad English and Czech from his Czech-born wife. He only tolerated those sounds in the bedroom.

Bijoux and her sexy little accent had been employed with the family for almost two years before they discovered she had a real gift for cooking. Taken off nanny duty, they put her to work in the kitchen, whereupon he insisted she wear a uniform befitting her new status in the household. Finally. It was perfect.

"I see you're looking well this morning too, Bijoux," he said as he turned his back on his family and dipped his finger into a bowl of yogurt left on the counter. Licking it off of his finger, he winked at her before turning back to his wife and daughter.

"Daddy! Can you take me to the studio this morning? I just love it when the other dancers see you; they're all so jealous that I have such a cool dad."

Hyde smiled broadly. "Sure, sure, I can do that. I've got a meeting in midtown anyway. Come on, let's go. Pravdina, when I get back, I want to meet with you and the stylist to go over your outfit choices for dinner tonight. Remember, we have the Packards tonight, and I need you to make an impression. Make sure everything is in order with Bijoux and the staff. It's just the four of us, at eight."

"Daddy!" Simone pouted. "When am I going to be able to join you for dinner. I'm old enough now to play hostess for you too."

Pravdina frowned at him as he adjusted his pants and belt, which were pinching him. He caught her look of annoyance as she turned to their daughter. "Simone!" she said. "You must hurry now, or you'll be late for class."

Simone stuck out her bottom lip in her mother's direction. Hyde smiled at his daughter's spunk and stunning retreating figure as she skipped out of the room. He turned to Prav and gave her a thumbs up. "You did a good job there with that one, Prav. I'll say this—you're a damn fine breeder!"

Hyde walked out. It felt great to be him.

THADDEUS BROTHERS, FOUNDING PARTNER of the well-heeled law firm of Brothers & Plimpton LLP, donned his usual patience as he met with his biggest client, Hyde Sutton. As usual, Thaddeus was piled over with work from his fat client, but this time with a wrinkle they hadn't seen coming. The subcontractors from Sutton Tower had organized, and they'd just received notice that a group of subs had secured representation from Baach, McKenzie & Blake. It was definitely a surprise.

"Those boys are big league, Thad. What do you think is going on here?" Hyde asked.

Thaddeus pushed his glasses up the bridge of his nose. "Just what it looks like, Hyde. They've organized and, somehow, sold it to the Baach boys. I'm not sure how they got in front of them, but since they did, I have to assume that Baach's taking it on commission. Which means, Baach thinks they have a case. The first papers came our way yesterday, demanding settlement, damages, threatening litigation, blah, blah, blah. How do you want me to handle it?"

Thaddeus momentarily averted his gaze as Hyde pushed back from the conference table and tugged his pants and belt over his burgeoning belly. The man's bloated face was oddly colored orange due to his spray tan. Up close, in the afternoon light, he looked like a melon about to burst.

"Let's get back to why they're doing this," said Hyde. "If Baach's so big, why would they take on something this small—relatively speaking? What—a couple of million bucks, maybe three on the table and, if they win something, which they better not," he poked his finger at him for emphasis, "maybe they net half a mil? I mean, I know that's a payday, but this is a small town. Why would they risk coming after *me* and just pissing me off?"

Thaddeus inhaled as he stared at his client of five years. He'd made good money representing Hyde Sutton, but it had come at the expense of his gray hair. Once again, he wondered what Hyde saw when *he* looked in the mirror. Thad was fairly confident it was nothing resembling the truth of a bloated man in his late sixties who dressed like a young boy in pea coats and any over-the-top whims of the designer of the month. "It's trending," Hyde had pumped back at him when Thaddeus once questioned his ensemble. Hyde had insinuated that Thad was seriously out of step. The insinuation would have been amusing if it hadn't been so stupid.

Thaddeus knew it was Hyde who'd earned that distinction. The man strutted through life like a peacock. The press loved him for it, and that never ceased to amaze Thad, who believed the phenomenon was akin to the emperor who wore no clothes. Everyone talked about Hyde's appearance, somewhat amused and excited to see what he'd do next, but no one said anything to his face. Hyde Sutton was far too vain to believe anything other than what he saw—and he clearly loved himself when he looked at his reflection in his pool of Narcissus.

The fact that he also believed he was a beloved figure in New York City was also a fiction he told himself, but Thaddeus was careful to avoid bursting that particular bubble. He was smart enough to realize that Hyde only surrounded himself with yes men and people who would support and flatter his world-sized ego. As long as his firm made money, Thaddeus would go along to get along.

Lost in retrospection and trying to form an honest-ish response, Hyde barked, "Who would do that? I'm the greatest thing that's ever happened to this city...to this country! I'm global! My name is known around the world, and these putzes think they can come after me? *Thad?* Maybe you're not doing your job? Maybe you're just not intimidating enough? Maybe I need to be looking for a bigger wolf here to represent me and my multi, multi, multi successful enterprises."

Thaddeus took off his glasses and squeezed the bridge of his nose. "Hyde, relax. I got this. It's just unusual, and I needed you to know. I wanted to confirm, in light of this new representation, that you wanted me to keep putting them off."

"Hell yes! We don't compromise. My word is my bond! And I gave these assholes my *word* that I would sue them until the end of days if they didn't just shut the fuck up and sit down."

Hyde put his short, fat finger in Thad's face. "No one comes after me. *No one can touch me.* I pay you huge amounts of money to make that happen, *Th, Th, Th,* Thad," Hyde stuttered in a mocking manner. "So just do your fucking job and make this go away. I've got to focus on the

St. Petersburg deal and the other big one in the Czech Republic. My time is too valuable for this shit. Little putzy, puking contractors...fucking carpenters and *plumbers* think they can touch me? I'm Hyde Sutton! Make this go away. Shut down the Baach boys today."

THAT EVENING HYDE LOUNGED in his penthouse study, going through some papers. Reclined in his desk chair, his velvet, monogrammed, slippered feet propped on his huge mahogany partners desk, he sat up when he saw a call coming in from Thad. He punched the answer button on his multiline house phone.

"Hyde," the lawyer's voice came through. "I thought you should know what I found out. We did some digging, and it turns out Baach isn't taking this thing on commission. Or rather, they are, but not in the traditional manner."

"What's that supposed to mean?" Hyde stood up and went to the window, running a hand through his hair as he admired his reflection in the glass. The long, satin smoking jacket, replete with pocket square and ascot was a good look for him.

"It means their payday is coming from another source. The Carrows family is funding the legal push, and Baach has been their go-to firm for years. Charlotte Carrows and Alex Macchi are behind it."

Hyde's mouth fell open as he turned from the window and then snapped it shut. "The Macchis? Why the fuck would they care about the subs?"

"I don't know, Hyde. But they're funding it, and I was told that they intend to take it the distance too—and we know how deep their pockets are."

"The Macchis?" He shook his head, squinting at the phone on his desk. "Simone takes dance class at the same studio with their daughter, Petunia. I see them all the time. Why are they getting involved here?"

"I don't know, Hyde. Do you have a good relationship with them? Do they dislike you for some reason?"

Hyde glanced again at his reflection in the glass. "Dislike me? What? Every time I see that Charlotte, I compliment her on her outfit. Every. Time. Even when I don't mean it. I make it a *point* to tell her how nice she looks. And she does look nice, that one. Real classy lady, maybe a little too buttoned up, but hey, she does it well. And the kid, Petunia? She's a real looker. Gonna be very, very pretty just like her mom. I told her that just the other day! What the fuck? The Macchis are coming for me? Like hell! You focus on making this go away. I don't want this lingering. Maybe give them a lowball offer, get it off the table."

"All right, Hyde."

Hyde disconnected the call and sat at his desk again. He looked around his opulent study and stared out at the Manhattan nightline—his fiefdom—wondering what this was all about. He punched speed dial #1 on his landline to his wife's cell. She answered from the other room.

"Pravdina! Get in here. I need to talk to you about Charlotte and Alex Macchi and see what you know about them. Now. And put on that new gold peignoir, maybe with those sexy slides from Bergdorf's. Stop in the kitchen along the way and bring me a bowl of those nuts Bijoux had at dinner tonight."

Hyde punched a button to disconnect and stared out the window. He could feel his blood pressure rise. "Charlotte Macchi. You nasty whore."

For the rest of the evening, among other activities, Hyde and Pravdina brushed up on the upcoming schedule of events at the Academy of Dance Arts. His Simone and the girls had a rigorous practice schedule gearing up for competitions, and Monday evening, there was a spirit committee meeting at the studio, which Hyde now knew was chaired by none other than Charlotte Carrows Macchi herself. He'd attend.

Chapter 4

CHARLOTTE NODDED HER THANKS and said her goodbyes to the other members of the spirit committee. With only a few weeks left in the season and the school year wrapping up, it was a busy time, but she loved every minute of it.

Alone in a long conference room at the dance studio, tidying up her space, she walked to a nearby trash can and disposed of some debris. Her head turned as she heard the unmistakable, booming voice of Hyde Sutton, somewhere nearby, outside the door.

"Gave her a thrill," he laughed. "The team's looking good!"

While not unheard of, Hyde Sutton didn't typically pick up his daughter from dance class. Charlotte's spider sense heightened as she realized that Hyde was most likely coming her way. She had to assume that he knew about the litigation threats against him and that she and Alex were helping to finance the effort.

"Hyde," she said casually, as his large body filled the open doorway. Holding a long—and what appeared to be sable—

coat, she caught his eye quickly and ascertained that he definitely had something to say before he'd move out of the way to let her pass. She continued gathering her bags of paraphernalia and kept her eyes on the task. She did not want a confrontation.

"Charlotte, you're looking well," he said coolly.

"Thank you. I'm just finishing up here if you need the room," she said as she bent over and grabbed the last bag.

Hyde didn't miss the moment and stuck his hand between her legs and squeezed her private parts hard.

Charlotte's heart lurched as she jumped up. She spun around and slapped out at him. "What are you doing! What the fuck do you think you're doing!"

Hyde smirked at her. "Doing what comes natural, baby, when a hot little number like you presents the goods."

Charlotte felt her face on fire, frantic with the situation and that someone had heard her yell out. She couldn't believe that he'd just assaulted her at her daughter's school! With every fiber of her being she wanted to knock the shit out of him and stand over his body, whaling on him, but she just stood frozen, astonished.

He rolled his shoulders and gave her a coy smile. Time slowed between them silently challenging each other, until she snapped out of it and realized she needed to get away from him. Her heart hammering, she roughly pushed past him into the hallway and went to the front desk, where several of the moms had gathered. Spying one of her friends, she tried to control her shaking and put her head down to hide her face. "Kelly, I need to run this stuff out to the car. I'll have Renzo come back to get Petunia."

Without looking up, she flew out to the waiting sedan

and piled in the back. She startled Renzo with the news of what had just happened as she worked to control herself.

"You want me to knock the shit out of him?" Renzo gave her a hooded look backed up by a seldom-seen, deeply menacing anger.

She rapidly shook her head. "No, but thanks for the thought. I'll speak with Alex. I just want to get home."

THAT EVENING, AFTER PETUNIA was out of earshot in her room and Lily was asleep, she pulled Alex behind the closed doors of their bedroom and sat cross-legged on the bed, while he took a chair across from her. She felt herself begin to shake as she told him what Hyde had done to her.

Alex's eyes looked like they were going to pop out of his head as he shot out of his chair. "He did *what?* Are you fucking kidding me?"

Charlotte put her hands over her face as waves of confusion washed over her. For the first time, she let it out and began to cry.

Alex knelt before her, pulling her into his arms. "Oh, God, Charlotte. I'm so sorry. I can't believe he did that. I'm so sorry. What can I do?"

She grabbed the back of his shirt warmed by his strength and let the tears fall. "Nothing...I don't know." She sniffed back a sob and inhaled deeply trying to compose herself. "What can we do? Women have to put up with this shit all the time." Wiping at her eyes, she felt her face contort again as another wave threatened. "But it was so vicious...and insulting."

Alex, his face red, sat back on his heels and clenched his jaw. "I want to fucking kill him. I'm not kidding here. He can't get away with this." He got up and paced.

Charlotte held her head in her hands, feeling sick. "Well he did, and I'm sure if I went to the police, it would be the talk of the town and, of course, my word against his. And what about Petunia? And the studio, and the girls? *Everyone* would be affected if I report this. His daughter, Simone—God, it would be a nightmare. Alex, I can't report him. No one can know about this, because it will hurt too many innocent girls, and I can't have that on my conscious."

He gave her an incredulous stare.

"He's such an animal," she snarled as she wiped her nose with the back of her sleeve.

Alex shook his head, his fists clenched. "Charlotte, I don't know. I mean, I understand that you're trying to protect Petunia, but goddamn it..."

He flicked his hands out at his side and stared at her, his eyes on fire. She shook her head no and pleaded for him to let it go through more tears.

He paced slowly in front of her. "Jesus. All right we won't go to the police. But for now, we're sure as shit going to do *something* to make him pay. We're going to dig into Hyde Sutton, look deep into his putrid life, and tear him apart. Don't try to stop me, Charlotte. After everything we've learned and now this? He's got it coming, one way or another."

Charlotte brushed the back of her hand against the streaks of mascara that had run down her face. "I won't stop you, Alex. I keep thinking about the look on his face afterward. Like he won or that he could do whatever he wanted to...like a bully just waiting to see if I would fight back. He's a monster. Who knows how many other people he's hurt? He thinks he can just get away with it."

Her nose tingled with another wave of tears as she reached out for Alex's hand. He came and sat next to her. She held his hands tightly as she looked into his soft, pained eyes. He was hurting too.

"Alex, listen to me. You've got to promise me we'll do this together, and you won't do anything you'll regret. Promise me you'll walk away from him if you see him in person. No punches or anything. That would only give him more satisfaction, and he'd definitely file charges. I'll be fine. *We'll* be fine. But I agree: He picked on the wrong girl and the wrong family. If he wants a war, he just got it."

They held one another, each with their own private thoughts. She mostly worried that Alex would be able to control his anger.

Chapter 5

AT THE BEGINNING OF ANY WAR, it's a good idea to get to know your enemy; so with that in mind, Charlotte and Alex called their favorite, highly illegal hacker extraordinaire, Bacon. But a man like Hyde Sutton, being a public figure, a businessman, a salesman, a con man, and a carnie barker—would come with much more information than they could manage themselves. They'd need help.

Also as usual, before waging their type of war, the extended Carrows family needed to be brought into the loop. Charlotte closed the door as she and Alex entered the modern, glassed-enclosed office of their rental apartment. She'd put Petunia in charge of baby Lily and now placed the dreaded conference call to her family. Charles, Angelica, and Carey in London, at the home in Curzon Square, and her parents in California were all told about Hyde Sutton and his actions.

Charlotte had been reluctant to bring her family into the mess. Only last month the family had gathered in California for the joyous wedding celebration of Charles and Angelica.

Everyone was still in high spirits with Angelica expecting twins, and she didn't want to drag them all through another sordid scandal. Not only that, but the family had just completed a not-without-fraught campaign against Gianluigi Rossini Rimini and his family in Italy. Alex had spent a great deal of time with Charles in London, protecting not only him, but the royal monarchy of Great Britain. It had been a strain on all of them.

But logic won out, and Charlotte and Alex grimaced their way through the tough conversation about her sexual assault.

"What kind of monster does that?" her mother yelled on the heels of the rest of the group's outrage. It felt good to hear their support, but it saddened Charlotte to hear their distress.

"We could be in New York tomorrow," said her father. "Anything you need. This is obscene."

"Thank you," Alex said, giving her a tender look. "But the only Carrows we might need would be Carey."

Carey said, "I'll help in any way I can. What an asshole! Angelica and I have a flight out to California in the morning to get her to mom and dads for the duration of the pregnancy. After I deposit her in California, I can come to New York."

Charles said, "Everything is finally under control here too. I'm just wrapping up a few things, but I was planning to travel to Vegas and Atlantic City. I was going to go back and forth to London between now and September, but I can absolutely make it out to New York if you need me as well."

Alex jumped in. "I appreciate everyone's offer to help and, believe me, we'll call you if there's anything you can do. Carey, if you could hang loose for a call, we'll let you know. In the meantime, we're waiting on Bacon for more information, and I've got my brothers, Michael and Tony, and some Macchi & Macchi agents working on it too. We'll pull what we need from whomever we need."

Alex rubbed his hands together. "Right now, we're still fact gathering, trying to figure out how to go at this guy. We've already gotten companies vetted who we believe have legitimate claims against Hyde from the Sutton Tower job, and once the word spreads, I have a feeling this could get big in a hurry. Hyde is going to be angry—already is angry, frankly, which is why I think he attacked Charlotte in the first place. With the litigation alone, assuming it goes to litigation, we're going to cost him millions."

Alex and Charlotte were distracted as they looked out through the glass and into the hallway as two-year-old Lily ran past, giggling, with Petunia following in her wake. "But there's a downside here," said Charlotte as she frowned and leaned toward the phone on the coffee table. "I'm afraid it's going to get really ugly, and I'm worried about the fallout on Petunia at the dance studio. If Simone Sutton is anything like her father, and I have a suspicion she might be, then she and her clique of girls might make life difficult for Petunia."

"Then get her out of there, Charlotte," her mom said tersely. "There are other studios in Manhattan. I know she loves that place, but if things get bad, you can move her out. She needs to be in a supportive environment, and I'm sure if the studio knew about the assault, they'd ask the Suttons to leave. You should tell them. And if they won't kick the Suttons out, then you need to protect her."

Charlotte hugged herself. "I'm not going to pull her now before the competition and recital season is over. She's part of a team, and all her friends are there. We already had a talk with her and told her that Alex and I were in a legal battle with Simone's dad. We asked her to let us know if anything screwy happens at the studio. I think she's prepared, but once again, it makes me upset that she might be affected by the grown-ups around her, making her life difficult. God knows she's already had enough of that to last a lifetime."

"Keep Renzo close to her," said Charles. "If you or Alex can't be around, keep some eyes on her. I also agree that you should have a talk with the academy director. At the bare minimum, let them know that there's a personal situation that might spill into the studio."

"It's a thought," Charlotte said reluctantly. "I just hate to get so many people involved. Maybe we should have predicted this when we got involved with the contractors."

"Charlotte," her dad admonished, "we don't ever back away from a good fight. We step up as one and will fully support you."

"All right," said Alex with resolve. "We'll consider speaking with the studio, and in the meantime, we'll keep tight eyes on the girls. We'll be in touch as the situation progresses, but don't worry, the Italian Macchis are fairly good at this revenge thing too."

JUNE

Chapter 6

REAMS OF INFORMATION WERE all over the conference table at the midtown-Manhattan warehouse offices of Macchi & Macchi. This particular part of the inner sanctum was for Macchi employees only. Clients never saw some of the sacred spaces. The Hyde war room had one wall covered in corkboard and another in white board; it was a visual mapping area where the teams gathered when complicated projects arose. There was more than one enclosed conference room in the warehouse offices, but this central one was the largest, most comfortable, and most secure. The entrance security codes changed as the room changed projects and personnel.

In the room now dedicated solely to Hyde Sutton, three of the Macchi brothers sat around the table, taking notes as their hacker reported in. Reports from Bacon were sent via encrypted e-mails and over highly secured lines and made communication secure. The room, too, was an electronically protected fortress. Bacon opened up the conversation in his nasal-toned, high-octave voice; he was in a jovial mood.

"Okay guys, I sent you a bunch of documents, all kinds of stuff. You're going to love this particular shit though. Get this: Hyde Sutton has had a few cases of *venereal disease*. Curable shit. Crabs. Holy shit. Crabs. Wow. I love this shit! Then there was some kind of bacterial yeast thing, which I don't even want to know about. What's pertinent, though, is that both were diagnosed and treated, I guess, since he's been married to Pravdina. So either he's been out doing something nasty with someone, or she has, or they both have. Whatever. But the next bit, the big kahuna, is that this dude has a penile implant. Yeah, says here that he got it 'cause he was having some trouble in the boudoir—or the whorehouse, more likely, if he was picking up crabs. Holy shit, I don't like thinking about that one, man.

"As for the rest of the shit I've been sending, you're going to need to narrow it down for me. I need something called *direction* here, you know. Too much information, only so much time. I actually got a life outside this shit, in case you were wondering, which frankly—never mind, don't wonder about me. Whatever. Tell me what you want, and I'll get it. As usual, get me his phone, laptop, files; that's where the good shit is stored."

Bacon disconnected. After a beat, Alex shook his head to clear it out and said, "Okay, I think that explains a lot about why he abuses women. He's gotta feel bigger than he actually is. I doubt Charlotte was the first woman he's assaulted. Maybe he resents them. We've seen enough of that lately."

Alex went to the whiteboard and started a list called Medical. He wrote crabs and penile implant under the column, then turned back to his brothers. "Bacon is right, though, we need to narrow this search.

"Let's look at Hyde's past projects, current projects, and future projects and focus on the people he's used: lawyers, contractors, and personnel who work for him in any capacity. We need to look at his lifestyle, his wife, his family, his assets, but most of all his businesses. He's crooked, so there'll be stuff here, we just need to find it. Let's split this up and bring in some help if we need it."

Michael, Alex's younger brother and partner, and Tony, his oldest brother and recently promoted police detective, sorted through the information. The three of them organized, pinning information, and throwing intel onto the boards around the room. Specifically, they looked for anything that popped up as unusual or illegal that could be used as leverage for Hyde Sutton's undoing.

They divided the workload, and over the next few days, a shape to the Sutton organization began to emerge as they developed a war board with the names of projects, property, people, and organizations. Hyde Sutton had a labyrinth of development deals, and it was crazy to discover that nearly every one of them had attached liens, lawsuits, and scandals—many of them even bankruptcies. The man had his stink and ruination on projects and people across the globe.

Chapter 7

As a cop, Tony, the eldest Macchi, knew that using a hacker was illegal. But being a Macchi first, he'd look away if his brothers and family needed him to.

Once he learned what Hyde Sutton had done to Charlotte, Tony began to use his spare time to work on the problem. He also knew his brothers were ethical people and that whatever information they gleaned from a hacker would be used for the right reasons. He knew Hyde Sutton was a corrupt businessman—on some level, everyone in New York did. Tony didn't like what he learned about Hyde screwing over the subcontractors, and while that might have been enough to justify breaking the hacking laws, he had no ethical problem about it all once Hyde assaulted his sister-in-law.

Tony Macchi loved his brothers. Many times they'd asked him to quit his job and join them at the firm, and while the bump in pay might be nice, he was living out another dream: finally achieving the goal of becoming a detective in the NYPD. He had two sets of family, and both were fighting the good fight. He was definitely torn, but for now, he chose to keep his cop job.

Digging into his assigned pile of assets owned by Hyde Sutton, Tony noticed that Hyde owned a warehouse complex on the Upper New York Bay near the Bay Ridge Channel and Belt Parkway. No information was in the files about the function of this warehouse, but Tony was intrigued. Marie Macchi, their mother, still lived in the home where she and Anthony Sr. had raised their family in the Bay Ridge area of Brooklyn. It happened that the warehouse in question was nearby.

That next Sunday, Tony, Abby, and their son, Riley, pulled up to his mom's modest four-bedroom home. Purchased by his parents in 1960 for $125,000, it was now worth close to $2 million. The three-story, narrow brick home was filled with family memories and the people who mattered most to him. He pulled into the long single driveway behind Alex's car and got out.

Looking toward the detached carport, he waved to Petunia, who was jumping rope with her cousins, Andria and Lauren. The three of them screamed for Riley to join them as Tony helped his pregnant wife out of the car and handed her a covered casserole—a shared dish she'd made for the regular Sunday meal.

He kissed her on the cheek. "You go inside, I gotta go check something out."

Abby cocked her head. "What, now? Where are you going?"

Tony shrugged. "Just something I gotta go look at for Alex. It shouldn't take long. I'll be back in thirty minutes or so."

"All right," Abby said as she walked up the sidewalk and toward the steps leading to the single front door. He waved and gave one last glance at Riley, who was safely being looked after by his cousins, and drove away.

As he drove toward the waterfront, he thought about what was happening with the investigation and his concern about Alex escalating the thing into a physical altercation with Hyde Sutton. He couldn't blame his brother for wanting to pummel the guy and recognized the importance of helping Alex find a different solution to his anger. He'd support the investigation in any way he could.

Alex was his little brother. A strong, capable guy who married well, Tony would always want to protect him. Alex could have become a complete dick after marrying into unbelievable money, but he was still the same guy. They'd talked about the money and what it meant a couple of times. Alex had told him that, above all, he wanted to remain the same person he'd always been. He primarily thought of the money as Charlotte's, but he also knew he could have just about anything he wanted. Yet what he wanted most, he'd said, was to help people and be remembered as a good man.

Tony admired him for it. He also knew a little bit about what Charlotte's family had done for their sister Isabella and for Finn. That was a debt he wouldn't take lightly either.

Something else he knew with certainty was that their mother would never want for anything. She had money of her own and the house, but it was good to know that the Macchis had a safety net. If shit happened, Alex would be there. And now, by God, he was going to be there for him—even if it meant breaking a few laws.

Tony drove the car close to the Sutton warehouse street and got out to walk the rest of the way. The east side of the street was lined with four- and five-story, nondescript buildings, while the west side had a tall security fence surrounding what appeared to be a complex of buildings and warehouses. He made one casual pass by the chain-link fence and looked at what he could see of the warehouse complex listed as an asset owned by one of Hyde's various companies. Having seen the property on Google Earth, he knew the warehouse had access to the water and the channel that led into and out of the harbor.

Growing up in Bay Ridge, kids spent a lot of their time watching the seagoing vessels enter New York Harbor from the Atlantic Ocean. The ships would cross through the lower bay through the narrows and into the upper bay, and the kids spent time letting their imaginations wander about where the different vessels had originated and what their purposes were in America.

Massive ships transporting hundreds of cargo containers entered the harbor every day and pulled into the terminals of the New York-New Jersey Harbor to deliver or receive their shipments. Because of their proximity to the water, it was a rite of passage for all the Bay Ridge kids to learn about the various maritime flags and their uses, from the flag announcing the country of registration to the house flag that identified which country owned the vessel. There was even an elective course in the Bay Ridge schools that covered the extensive history of admiralty law.

He knew quite a lot about the harbor and had friends who were Port Authority cops. If he hadn't known before, since 9/11, he and every cop in New York understood the risks that came from the harbor. The vastness of it—the third largest harbor in the nation—meant the Coast Guard protected it with gunboats, holding precision marksmen at the ready. Of the roughly 1,400 daily vessel movements in the harbor, about 250 were deemed sensitive areas, and the Coast Guard focused where the risk level was highest.

Since 9/11, all vessels coming into the harbor were required to give a ninety-six-hour notice of arrival. A list of crew and cargo had to be provided, and random inspections could take place as much as twelve miles offshore, often in the middle of the night.

Having seen what he could from the front of what appeared to be a vacant complex, Tony walked down the side street and toward the water to see if he could get a better look at the setup in the back. Unable to get a good idea from that vantage point either, he tried various points of entry to see if he could get through the fence and into the complex. He knew he was taking a risk of trespassing as he climbed over a lower section of the fence that seemed to present a blind spot to the rest of the complex. Dodging in-between the buildings, he eventually found a place that gave him a clear look at the back of the buildings and the pier, as well as several vans and cars parked behind one of the buildings.

As he looked around, he was puzzled to see no signage of any kind. The property complex was listed as Bay Ridge Properties, an asset of the Mercer Investment Group and owned by Hyde Sutton. It was clearly being used for something, but for what was unclear. The buildings, the vans, the cars, the fences, nothing seemed to indicate who owned the property or its purpose. Trying to decide whether to venture closer or go back, Tony felt an impact, and his body hit the ground. After that, he didn't remember anything.

ALEX TRIED TO STOP FIDGETING and appear calm as he sat with Michael, Abby, and Lauren in the New York Methodist emergency room while they waited for the doctor's update on Tony's condition.

After his brother didn't reappear at their mother's home and was unresponsive to calls, they'd begun to worry. Abby explained that Tony didn't tell her where he was going, only that he needed to check on something nearby for the project he was helping them on.

Alex swallowed back his sick fear that his brother's disappearance may have something to do with their work. Due to the volume of paperwork they'd parceled out, he wasn't sure which property Tony was visiting. Just as they'd made the decision to hit the streets and look for him, Abby got a call from the Methodist emergency room, informing her that Tony was being treated for injuries he sustained in what was thought to be a mugging.

With the rest of the family waiting on pins and needles at home, the four Macchis rose as a doctor in scrubs finally approached to give them the news.

"Mr. Macchi, or Detective Macchi as I've come to understand, was found on the side of the road not far from the parkway and was unresponsive at the scene. The ambulance brought him here, and he regained consciousness. He's suffered a head trauma and is having scans to determine the extent of the injuries. He also suffered a broken wrist, possibly from the fall, and some facial lacerations. Once he's back from radiology, we'll bring you back to see him, and we'll know more at that time."

"Was he able to speak with you? Did he tell you what happened?" Alex asked.

The physician looked at the women. "He was speaking, but only asked for his wife."

Alex felt his gut clench as Abby covered her mouth. Lauren supported her as the doctor continued, "He was apologizing to you and wanted to make sure you knew he loved you. He was somewhat unfocused, however, so we needed to get to radiology quickly."

Abby began to cry, and Lauren put her arm around her.

"Someone will be out to get you as soon as he's back in the room, Mrs. Macchi." The doctor gave them a professional nod and left.

Alex tried to comfort his sister-in-law. "Abby, Abby, this is good news. He's going to be okay. I'll call the rest of the family and let them know what's going on. Michael, could I have a word with you?" Alex pointed to another empty waiting area nearby. "We'll just be over there and will be right back."

After calling Charlotte at his mom's house to give them the update, Alex ran a hand through his hair and turned to his brother. "Michael—shit. Do you think this had something to do with the Hyde project?"

Michael crossed his arms. "It had to be. Abby said he was going to check out something for us, so it wasn't a cop-related job."

"Do you think it could have been a random mugging?" Alex lowered his voice.

"I don't know. Maybe. I'm sure the cops will talk to us soon enough. Off duty or not, they'll go into overdrive to figure out what happened to him."

Alex glanced over at Abby and Lauren. "Jesus, I feel so guilty. I didn't see this coming, did you? Violence like this? What could he have seen for someone to attack him?"

"Well, we won't know if it's related or not until we talk to him. I hope he won't bring the Hyde Sutton investigation into his interview with the cops. But then, God knows I'm not going to stop my brother from telling the truth."

Alex blinked. "No, of course not. My only concern is for him and the family, you know that. Let's get back and tell Abby that Mom's on her way."

MUCH LATER, IN THE MIDDLE of the night after Tony had been admitted to a room, and Marie and the rest of the family had been encouraged to leave and get some rest, Alex and Michael stood at their brother's bedside. They looked into his swollen, stitched-up face and came to terms with the news that Tony had sustained a grade 3 concussion. Mercifully, the scans showed no signs of bleeding in the brain. His wrist would need reparative surgery, but the doctors were waiting until the morning when the head of orthopedics would arrive to perform the operation. Tony was heavily sedated, but not cognitively impaired. The brothers had been waiting to speak with him alone.

"Tony," Alex said softly in the darkened room, "I'm so sorry this happened to you. We're all so grateful you're going to be okay."

Tony mumbled, speaking through his pain. "I told the cops what I know. I didn't see them. Anyone. They must have hit me from behind."

"They said you were mugged. Do you think that's true? Did they steal anything?" Alex pressed his opportunity.

"My wallet is gone."

"Okay, what about your badge?"

"Left the badge. Don't know why."

"Tony," said Michael, "I'll get onto your credit cards and cancel them. Don't worry about that."

"Not worried about that."

Alex said, "Do you remember where it happened? What were you doing?"

"Checking out Bay Ridge Property. Hyde. Warehouse. Got a dock. I went over the fence, and it happened in there."

Alex gripped the bedside rail. "Jesus. And they dumped you outside? Outside of the property?"

"Cops said they found me by the parkway. Yeah. Outside."

"You think this was random, or was something to do with the property and Hyde?"

Tony didn't answer. He closed his eyes and looked as if he drifted off before coming back to them. "Hyde. Not random. Something at warehouse."

Alex raised his chin and shot Michael a piercing glance before continuing, "Okay, Tony. That's enough for now. Listen, you rest now. The doctors will be here in a few hours to take you up to surgery. You're going to be good as new. Michael and I will be with you all night, and Mom and Abby will be over in a few hours to see you before they wheel you away."

"Riley?"

"Riley's with Lauren and the girls, Tony," said Michael. "He's just fine. Nothing to worry about, okay? You get some sleep now."

They watched Tony close his eyes and then left the room.

Alex looked down the quiet, sterile hall, almost bursting with regret and anger. He rubbed his hand roughly over his mouth. "We gotta find out what happened to him. I'm sure the cops are going to interview the people at the warehouse, but I want Bacon to focus on that property. I'm going to head over there today and have a look around."

"He got lucky, Alex. You know that right? Whoever did this, maybe the badge stopped them. He was trespassing, though, and whoever did this was also inside the fence line, so it's gotta be related to the place. You be careful."

"I wanna kill him," Alex mumbled, his jaw clenched, his head down.

"Don't be an idiot," Michael said, then added, "Fuck it. We'll do it together."

Chapter 8

SEVERAL DAYS LATER, Alex sat in a chair in Tony's living room and felt his jaw clench as his brother grimaced in pain. Abby and Riley were out, and this was the first real opportunity Alex had to be with Tony alone since the attack. Reclining in his own chair, Tony was recovering, but sporting a large cast on his arm.

"They need me back at work. The time off is rough on my caseload. I'm sorry, Alex. I'm just really pressed. I gotta get back."

The sight of his brother's battered face sickened him, but he tried to keep things light. "Listen, don't worry about it. We've got Karla Fernandez working the war room, and she'll get it organized if anyone can. We'll take care of it. We're just glad you're alive."

"Yeah, I'm alive, but they could have killed me, Alex. You gotta watch your six. The cops said they interviewed a guy at the warehouse. I'll get you a copy of the report. No one there saw nothin' that night. The cops were treating him like a potential witness because of the proximity, but there are no cameras in the area—so for good or bad, the cops got nothing on that end. If they did see me trespassing on camera, well, then the cops might see this thing in a different light. I didn't tell them I was inside the fence when it happened, so I lied and that doesn't feel good. But I couldn't tell them what I was doing in there, breaking the law, in the first place."

Alex looked down, his head swimming with conflicting thoughts, and then back into his oldest brother's swollen eyes. "So where does the investigation stand with them?"

"I don't know. They're going to keep asking questions, knocking on doors, but it doesn't look like any witnesses are going to step up, so that could lead nowhere."

"It made the news, so it's possible that someone saw something," said Alex.

"Not if the neighborhood knows better than to say something. The cops haven't gotten anywhere with the locals."

"If it's related to Hyde, then we'll find out."

"What are you planning to do?" asked Tony.

"I went over and took a look at the place, and I saw the problem with the layout and the fence: you can't see anything from the street. However, I did notice that directly across the street it's lined with office buildings. It so happens there's a five-story one that has a wonderful view of the warehouse and the pier behind it. We've rented a space on the top floor, and I've got Santiago and Josh up there, keeping an eye on the complex. Also, we got a report from Bacon on that specific property, but didn't find out much other than it's owned by one of Hyde's holding companies, the Mercer Investment Group."

Tony nodded. "Yeah, that's right."

"According to Bacon, the property was purchased by Hyde way back in the 1990s and has mostly been sitting vacant, just looking good on a spreadsheet as part of his real estate holdings. I assume he'd like to develop it, but he's either been too busy with his other projects or hasn't found the right deal to offload the property. Hyde—or technically Mercer Investment Group—pays the taxes on the place, but we can't find any income associated with the property. If he's subleasing it, he's not reporting it, or it's buried in paperwork somewhere."

"What do you think you're going to find over there, Alex?"

"Maybe nothing. I don't know, but someone beat the crap out of you and then threw you outside of the place. I mean, why go to those extremes? They could have called the cops and told them there was a trespasser. They also could have just waited for you to leave, but instead they muscled up hard and took you out. They, obviously, didn't want an investigation on the property or to give the cops a reason to ask what you might have been looking for. So they had to dump you outside the fence line to protect whatever is happening inside."

"One thing I can tell you," said Tony, "is the cops had trouble finding someone to interview because most of them only spoke Russian."

"Really? *Russian.* Well that's interesting. We'll keep that in mind."

Tony frowned and lowered his voice. "I want to get them as much as you do, but listen to me. Tread softly, brother. Don't go and do something stupid, you hear? That won't do any of us any good."

Alex nodded, but looked away. He wouldn't make any promises.

Chapter 9

DESPITE THEIR AGE DIFFERENCE, Roman Timofeyev was one of Hyde Sutton's best friends. Purposefully. A mutually advantageous courtship between the two men had begun nearly three years ago. They'd met at one of the many toney charity events intended to keep the wealthy New Yorkers comingling and networking the pants off each other. The one-upmanship of the charity world and being a proper "who's who" in the stream of circulating gossip helped the elite reassure one another of their place in society. Hyde and Pravdina Sutton attended as many events as possible for exactly that reason, as did Roman. It was his job as his father's cultured front man.

Only twenty-eight, Roman had ingratiated himself into Hyde's inner circle and introduced him to his father's network of Russian oligarchs working the angles to set up shop in the Big Apple. Roman had impressed Hyde, who was surprised that Roman was from Russia since he spoke with a slight British accent, which he explained had been acquired because he'd been raised in a British boarding school.

After meeting, the two spent time together, flexing their muscles and playing the "I'll show you mine if you show me yours" game. Hyde's game, Roman immediately recognized, came with his desperate need to feel superior at all times, so he pretended to believe it. He was no fool and realized it greased the wheels of their relationship.

But Roman wasn't hanging around Hyde for the awkward, often difficult, one-sided friendship. Eventually, getting to the heart of the matter, he'd asked Hyde to invest in two of his property development plans in St. Petersburg and Prague. Real estate development deals were right up Hyde's alley. When their lawyers were brought into the meetings to move the ball forward, Hyde was finally exposed to the fact that Roman was really working for his father, Viktor Timofeyev. As a silent partner, there was a reason his father kept a low profile. He wasn't—nor did he ever want to be—the "right kind of people."

Roman's father, Viktor, lived and prospered quietly in Brighton Beach, but anyone who chose to look closer would discover that he was a dangerous man. Over the years, Roman had witnessed and learned much about his colorful, brutal, and powerful father. People feared Viktor and his violent past, and Roman lived quite happily in the wake of his father's notoriety.

Born in 1968, Viktor Timofeyev rose to power in the Soviet Union during the zenith of Soviet sports and Mikhail Gorbachev's *perestroika* reforms. He was a decorated Master of Sport, a national award given to him for medaling in boxing, and part of the great Soviet push for athletic greatness that encouraged USSR athletes to obtain brute strength. But those programs fell apart, leaving the dangerously trained men to roam the streets and form the gangs of athletes who ruled St. Petersburg from 1992 to 1996.

After his dreams of athletic glory came to an end, Viktor became a bouncer and worked as an enforcer for his gang. Known as "The Arm," his extreme strength became legendary at one particular "*Strelki*" meeting where racketeering gangs came to resolve business disputes. He made a name for himself as a smart, brutal risk taker and didn't spend all of his money on drink, whores, and drugs like so many of his associates. He used it wisely, and the heavily tattooed enforcer was, eventually, brought to America where he continued to use his brawn and his brain to prosper.

Viktor fathered Roman before leaving Russia at age twenty, but left him behind to be raised by his mother. The drug-addicted woman, for whom Roman now felt only ambivalence, began dying of liver failure when Roman was ten—a fact that finally forced Viktor to take parental responsibility. If his father didn't take him, Roman would be abandoned to a St. Petersburg orphanage.

Not the fatherly type, Viktor nevertheless did the right thing and came to St. Petersburg to meet him for the first time. It was a meeting Roman remembered vividly. Roman had been left to his own devices by his mostly absent mother and had learned about life on the streets, not in school. The day of his father's arrival, Roman had cleaned the small, filthy apartment and made certain to show respect to the large, domineering man who had finally shown up. Roman recognized the tentative nature of the visit, but it was his opportunity to finally get something from the man. He wasn't going to let him leave without a commitment to help.

Roman did what he could to sell himself, hoping for a ticket to America and a job with his father, but Viktor had his own plans. He arranged for Roman to leave Russia all right, but he sent him to a military school in Britain. There, he told his son, he would become educated and polished and one day be of value to him in the world he was building in America.

Initially angry with his father's distasteful plan and fearful that he would fail, Roman surprised everyone, including himself, by thriving. He worked hard to catch up with his academics, and his street smarts gave him the ability to maneuver the other boys to either befriend or fear him. Most chose friendship, while some kept their distance, but they all had to choose. Roman also reveled in his travels, eating up the exciting summers he spent with his father in New York. Those visits reinforced the fact that he had a bright future ahead of him if he kept himself out of trouble. And his father insisted upon it. He could keep his grades up and stay out of trouble or he could go back to the streets of Russia. He too, had to choose.

When he graduated from NYU with a degree in real estate, Roman never looked back on his early years, and he never regretted his choices. He and his father became partners in every way, but Roman knew it was, and always would be, Viktor who controlled their destinies.

After Hyde Sutton was thoroughly groomed and seated at the deal-making table, they'd reached an inevitable juncture. After the legal disclosures and Viktor's participation became clear, Hyde told Roman he wanted to meet his father. Viktor gave the okay, but only after the business partnership on the hotel and convention resorts in St. Petersburg and Prague were finalized and signed.

THE DAY OF THE MEETING ARRIVED; Roman heard the door slam and his father call, "Timo," as he walked through the front door. Roman rushed to the door, uncharacteristically nervous that the big get-together was happening, and greeted Viktor, who handed him a large bag.

"For safe," his father said as he walked past him into the living room.

"I've got another tray for the table. I'll be right back."

Roman walked quickly for the kitchen and dumped the bag on the counter, opening it briefly to peer inside. Cash. He turned to grab the last tray of hors d'oeuvres and walked toward the living room. His father didn't enjoy elegant restaurants or blending in, but that didn't mean the man didn't expect a good meal. The venue for the Sutton meeting needed certain privacy restrictions, and so, for the first time, Roman had invited Hyde to his home in Brooklyn.

Walking back into the living room, Roman placed the last tray among a pile of food on the coffee table.

"This is good spread," his father nodded vigorously as he dug in.

Roman felt pleased as he sat near his father, quietly observing the man's powerful presence in his home and soaking up the confidence Viktor always exuded. Peacefully enjoying the food with sincere pleasure, one might be lulled by the innocent gaiety Viktor had while eating, but one should look closer.

Although his father had lost much of the muscle mass from his athletic youth, he was still a huge bear of a man, heavily tattooed with a strong Russian accent and no interest in making a false impression on those he met. He looked exactly like what he was: an old-school Russian enforcer, menacing and foreign. He always wore a mustache to hide his badly stained and crooked teeth. Although he could easily afford the cosmetic and dental work to achieve a perfect smile, Viktor liked what he saw in the mirror. His refusal to change served to remind everyone of his background. His love of gold chains, which he still believed reflected his good taste and material wealth, were also on display to reflect his high status. No one, especially not Roman, presumed to tell him otherwise. Besides, his father's appearance was a deeply effective package that people, heedfully, responded to. It all worked.

"Zasha made awful Olivier salad last night. Bologna. I tell her no more. She make up for in other ways." Vikor smiled as he stuffed a small dessert blini with mascarpone into his mouth.

Roman didn't care much for his father's latest girlfriend. This one owned a nail salon and had trinkets imbedded and hanging from a few of her long nails. His father had never married, telling Roman that women would just spend his money in ways that didn't interest him. Instead, he had a long stream of women in his life and counseled Roman to live by the same principles. Roman dutifully listened and complied.

"She still have that awful cat?" Roman asked, having unexpectedly encountered the almost feral animal at the salon some months ago while on an errand for his father.

"She say it is bad luck to return to street. Too late. Never leaves salon."

Roman thought about Zasha with distaste, recalling her pierced tongue and elaborately teased-up hair. His father would never participate in the conventional lifestyle of the American culture. He remained unaffected by the trappings of his wealth, still living in a modest home. Given his wardrobe, his lust, and his appetites for the darker sides of life, he would never blend in. Viktor was entirely comfortable letting Roman manage their public image, and the arrangement worked wonderfully for them both.

To that end, Roman lived quite well in a nice, newly renovated, four-story townhome in Brooklyn overlooking Prospect Park. While not a Manhattan address, it afforded him closer proximity to his father and more living space for half the cost of real estate on the other side of the East River.

Roman glanced around his surroundings, wondering what the snobbish Hyde would think and nervously rubbed his hands together while they waited for him. "So remember, Dad. Hyde Sutton expects to be treated like the most important person in the room. It's how I play him, remember?"

Viktor snorted and waved a dismissive hand. "You too nervous, Timo. Not like you. We are Timofeyev."

Roman couldn't disagree with any of that, but then, having his father and Hyde Sutton in the same room would be like watching two silverbacks catch eyes for the first time. Both would expect dominance. It made him uneasy.

The bell interrupted and Roman rose. He licked his lips. "Here we go, Dad. You ready?"

Viktor waved at hand at him. "Open door, Timo. I manage this man."

Roman turned toward the door, not at all confident the two men would play nice.

Viktor Timofeyev sat comfortable in his son's living room, helping himself to the wonderful spread of caviar, toasts, and the ever-present iced vodka as his son escorted the famous Mr. Hyde Sutton into the room. He'd seen enough press on the man to understand two things: Hyde was rich and a mover/shaker. He could get deals done and make them money, which was all Viktor needed to know. Roman had warned him the man was difficult, but Viktor had never met anyone he couldn't control.

"Dad, this is Hyde Sutton. Mr. Sutton, my father, Viktor Timofeyev."

Viktor stood and assessed his new partner, not quite believing what he saw. Hyde Sutton was wearing black pants and a long, single-breasted Nehru jacket with large silver buttons and a big poufy silver pocket square on his chest. He looked like he should be a performer in some odd Chinese theater.

"Mr. Timofeyev," Hyde said, reaching over the coffee table to shake his hand. "Nice to meet you. You mind if I call you Viktor? Mr. Timofeyev's a bit of a mouthful. You can call me Hyde."

Viktor nodded his head and was about to speak, but Hyde plowed forward in conversation. "So, hey, what do you think of my jacket? Putin wore one like this just the other day, and I said to myself, *Hey that man has some class*, so I had my guy get one for me."

Hyde posed, doing a half turn and then back. "If you like, I can put you in touch with him. Very elegant clothes. Very elegant. Expensive. Nothing but the best. But hey, I don't need to tell you that. Roman here, he's practically on the best-dressed list all the time. You've got a great son here."

Hyde put his hands up before him and spread his fingers. "The first time I met him, I said to myself, *Now there goes someone who knows how to make a good first impression.*

No kidding. His mother must have been a real looker, and you, obviously, too, 'cause Roman is a real ladies' man."

Viktor glanced at his son with his high cheekbones, square chin, and squinty blue eyes. Very much resembling his mother, the boy had not inherited much from him, other than his keen intelligence and predatory nature.

"So, hey," Hyde continued as he walked away from Viktor and turned his attention to the walls in his son's home. "Nice place you have here, Roman. Very nice...for Brooklyn. You got what—3 or 4,000 square feet?"

"Just about five." Roman said.

"You got a garage in this thing too?"

"Yes." Roman said, glancing at his father, who had yet to say one word.

"So hey, what's this set you back? Two, three mil?"

"Closer to four after the renovations." Roman nodded politely.

"Very nice," Hyde pronounced as he slapped Roman on the back and walked over to the coffee table. He sat in a side chair, and Viktor resumed his seat on the sofa. "So what've we got over here, some caviar? Love it. The Russians, now they have some nice caviar. You ever tried the Iranian Beluga? Pravdina and I, we served it the other night when we had the mayor and his wife over for dinner. Woof, woof on that one, am I right? You see that broad? Her backside gets bigger every year, and she dove into that caviar, let me tell you. We spent, what, probably thousands on it, though, so nothing but the best for the two of them. Gotta keep those politicians happy." He leaned forward in his chair, picked up a cracker, and scooped up a large portion of caviar.

While Hyde took a breath to chew and swallow, Roman got in, "What can I get you to drink?"

"Diet Coke? Diet Pepsi, whichever is fine." Hyde chewed and swallowed as he wiped the crumbs off his hands onto the floor and pointed at Viktor. "So, Viktor, Roman tells me you live in Brighton Beach. How long you been over there?" Hyde looked down at the spread and picked up a toast point. He scooped some caviar onto it and picked up a bowl of egg yolks. He poured some on top, sprinkling the table with droppings, before shoving the entire toast into his gaping mouth.

Viktor rested his arms on his legs and let his hands fall between them. "I've been there since I arrived from St. Petersburg. Various places, but neighborhood suits me." Viktor glanced at Roman, who grimaced.

"I can see that. What do you do over there?" Hyde chewed with his mouth open.

Not that he'd had a chance to get them in, but Viktor felt a bit lost for words while watching Hyde Sutton puff up his chest and take charge. He was grateful that Roman had prepared him to expect to be insulted. Having seen his share of just about everything in life, he was still amazed by the force of this man's exuberant overconfidence and dominant character, all while wearing silly clothes.

"This and that. Roman and I, we have business together." Viktor said softly.

"I see. So you're a part of the St. Petersburg and Prague deals, right?"

"I am." Viktor sat back, his legs spread wide, his hands clasped in his lap.

"Are you planning on traveling that way with us when we go over there soon?"

"No, I prefer to stay in United States. There are some

people in St. Petersburg who might not be interested in seeing me."

"Uh huh. So, Roman, he's my man? I won't be doing the day to day with you, but with Roman. That's right?" Hyde's tongue probed his teeth as he looked over to Roman.

"That's correct," said Viktor.

"So you won't be doing any press events over there, or over here for that matter, when we get ready to launch?"

"Correct."

Hyde threw his hands in the air. "Well, I can handle that for all of us, anyway. It's really one of my strengths. People love to hear me talk. Really. All the time. They clamor to all of my press conferences, so the media, that part and the publicity, my team will be on top of that. And I have the best team. The best in the industry. If you need help with public relations or the press, my people, everyone wants my people to represent them. I'll put in a word for you. There's this girl over there, I always ask for her exclusively. She loves me. The ass on her, let me tell you, a ten." Hyde splayed his fingers. "All she has to do is walk into a room, and she has the attention of everyone in it. Not like my wife, Pravdina, of course. I mean, that's world-class ass, but this one, she's out there—she knows what she's doing."

The meeting went on in this fashion as Hyde Sutton held court, believing he was entertaining them, until he suddenly stood and announced that he had another engagement.

Shaking Viktor's hand vigorously, Hyde said, "It was a real pleasure to meet you, sir." He put his hand on Viktor's back and gestured for him to walk with him. Hyde guided him around the coffee table as if he were a child and toward the front door as he continued to babble. Viktor was unaccustomed to people touching him without permission, but allowed the arrogant man to believe he was leading.

"Remember what I said about my tailor or my PR firm. I'd love to put you two together. It's what I do. I bring people together everywhere I go. Roman, thanks for having me. If you ever need a place in the city, be sure to let me know. My team of realtors? The best. The very best in Manhattan. So we'll be in touch. I think our properties in St. Pete's and Prague are going to be huge. I've got a tremendous gift for finding the right development deals and bringing the right people together. This thing is going to make us a lot of money. A lot of money."

After seeing Hyde out, Roman returned to the room and looked at him. Viktor's mouth hung open in astonishment. "My God. Man never shut up. You deserve bonus, Timo, for putting up with that jackass. Man's a legend—he's got that right—but I think it might be for different reasons than he thinks."

"He has been known to take advantage of his partners, Dad," Roman cautioned.

Viktor stared at his son and looked around at the pile of debris Hyde left on the table. "There is no reason to worry on that front, Timo. Let Mr. Hyde believe he is controlling us, running show, if it makes him happy. We are patient. We will use him when we need him, when we choose. We are in business for long game, Timo, not for short deal. We can be patient. My God, you will need to be very patient."

Chapter 10

Hyde sat in his Sutton Tower office and read through Page Six of the *Post* while he contemplated his visit with the Timofeyevs. His attorney, Thaddeus Brothers, cautioned him that Viktor Timofeyev was not a man to be trifled with. Thad had told him several times that he was uncomfortable with the dangers of entering into a business arrangement with Roman and Viktor; however, Hyde assured him that Viktor was just a paper tiger and the deals were really with the very cultured and elegant son, Roman. Viktor, he'd explained, was deep in the background, and Thad shouldn't be such a wimp. Business was business was business was busi-ness, and Hyde was good at it. He was getting sick of Thad.

Hyde did have some awareness of the volatility of the Russians, however, and even though it wasn't his style, he decided to stop short of screwing over Roman on their deal...just in case. At least for now. Besides, the deals would be huge. Viktor Timofeyev had made an impression on him though. Peripheral, but enough for Hyde to understand that Thad had a point.

He was highly pleased about his terrific relationship with the Russian oligarch set. Others may not have the balls to deal with them, but he sure did. Bit by bit, over the course of the last two years, he and Roman had grown closer and comingled in more and more schemes. In big ways and small ones, they helped one another, and their St. Petersburg and Prague developments were coming along nicely. They were the crown jewels in both of their development caps, and neither one wanted anything to upset their potential success.

Dropping the *Post*, he picked up another paper, always keeping a close eye on the action in his city, but stopped reading when he saw an article about a cop who'd been mugged near a warehouse in Bay Ridge. The only reason the article even jumped out at him at all was because the name of the victim was Tony Macchi, and the name *Macchi* was high on his list of special interests. The name of the of the warehouse stood out too. He owned it.

"What the fuck?" he mumbled.

During his budding relationship with Roman, he'd asked the Russian to become a partner in the Mercer Investment Group, which held various real estate assets around New York City and New Jersey. He used the book value of the Mercer Investment Group as collateral to raise money from banks and other investors on his projects.

The Mercer Investment Group owned the speculative complex of warehouses in Bay Ridge known as Bay Ridge Properties. As majority owner of the Mercer Investment Group, he'd given Roman permission to use the property until, or if, a use of the crumbling property meant they could pull it out of the portfolio of Mercer for sale. For the last two years, Roman had used the warehouse for private purposes. Hyde could have cared less what they did with it, but this information raised his hackles.

He called Roman and told him to meet him for lunch.

Hyde chose a busy restaurant near Central Park West, where he was on friendly terms and made sure they were sitting in the middle of the restaurant, at high noon. Wearing a gray-cashmere suit jacket with black ribbing on the collar and pockets, his white dress shirt was unbuttoned to below his sternum and another sheer black shirt showed underneath. His feather-light silk tie was knotted in a loose, untraditional manner and hung below his waist and was getting in the way. It, unintentionally, landed on the table.

Hyde glanced down at the long black tie and brushed it to the side as he continued his conversation with Roman. "So this cop, this off-duty cop, did you hear about it," Hyde said as he finished swallowing. "His name is Tony Macchi. He was mugged over there in Bay Ridge by the waterfront. Did you hear about it?"

Hyde stopped to shovel some salad dripping with blue cheese into his mouth. Not waiting for Roman to answer, he pointed his fork in Roman's direction and continued, "Because that asshole, that cop, he's a Macchi. Brother of Alex Macchi and he deserved whatever he had coming to him. I told you about them trying to come for me, right? Dumb fucks. They think they can just walk into my negotiations and take over; they got another think coming. That's what I'm telling you. They're dumb fucks. I hate those Macchis—and the Carrows too. They think they're really something special. You should meet them sometime.

"We go way back, the Carrows family and me. I did a few deals with the dad, Henry, out in California. Let me tell you, that man's a world-class idiot. And the daughter, Charlotte? She married a total loser: middle class for the love of God! Billionaire woman lands a middle-class guy. I ask you, what's that about? Why'd she hook up with *that* guy? From Brooklyn? It doesn't make any sense at all. She could've married money, real power, but no, she's with this little asshole, nobody Italian family from Brooklyn."

Hyde speared some steak and chewed vigorously as he continued his vitriol against the Macchi and Carrows families while Roman dutifully listened. "So, that warehouse, right over there in Bay Ridge, you're still using that right? 'Cause we need to keep it clean over there; you know what I'm saying, no bullshit now. Don't be a dumbass, Roman, that's all I'm telling you. No attention drawn to us; we've got these deals going, and they're going to be great. The greatest. I'll make you richer than you could have ever dreamed. You and your father. You stick with me, I'm telling you, and you'll go places. You and your father are lucky you met me, but keep me happy."

Hyde stopped and gave Roman a harsh, steely eyed look.

Roman shrugged. "You've got nothing to worry about, Hyde. I'll look into it."

Good enough. *Tony Macchi. What a dumb fuck.*

RIDING IN THE BACK of his town car, Roman let out a groan of frustration and shook his fist. As usual, his meeting with Hyde had been taxing, and he'd let him ramble. The luncheon took much longer than necessary due to Hyde grabbing the attention of anyone who looked his way. Roman was also annoyed when the man finally heaved himself out of his chair and left him with the fat check.

Roman went directly to his father in Brighton Beach to tell him about the conversation.

Viktor said, "Man is truly amazing; he thinks he is actually giving us Timofeyevs leg up. You do good job taking his shit, Timo."

"Thanks. It's not easy. He's an incredible boor with absolutely no sense of humor. Everyone knows it, but they put up with it because he's one of them. One of the 'it crowd.' He's an inside joke, but people are still willing to deal with him."

"You do good work, Timo."

"So the warehouse...anything to worry about over there? Maybe we should cut back on the shipments, skip a month or something until things cool down?" Roman knew perfectly well what had been going down there for the last two years.

"No, we go ahead. This is our port of entry, and Hyde left it laying around, doing nothing with safe pier. We use it. Nothing to worry about. You just keep Mr. Hyde on track and projects going forward; let me worry about warehouse."

"What if he asks more questions about it?"

"Then shut him down. You both go to Russia soon. This will keep him busy. It's too late for him to pull out of our deals. Business will be too profitable. He pulls out, he must know we would kill him. No, he won't do that. You keep me in loop, and if he steps off path, I can bring him back in line. Do not worry, Timo, Mr. Hyde will play."

Roman didn't want to argue. His father always did what he wanted. "Whatever you say."

Viktor nodded. "Yes. This is what I say."

Chapter 11

"I DON'T LIKE GOING TO THE STUDIO; the women stare at me," Pravdina argued. Since the Macchis had made their play against him, Hyde worried they might be bad-mouthing them to the other influential families; he wanted her inside with her ear to the ground and found her whining tiresome. "I don't give a hot holy shit what *you* don't like about it. We need to stay on top of the gossip. It's your duty as a Sutton. They're all just jealous of us."

Pravdina's pouty mouth turned down further, and she turned to walk away. His eyes, as usual, landed on her magnificent ass. Her best asset. "I tell you what, Prav. How about I take over. It's not like I have anything else to do," he called. She angrily waved a hand in the air and kept going. That gesture might have been enough, but then she flipped him the bird.

"What a bitch," Hyde mumbled. He sniffed, considered his options, and pulled out his cell, placing a call to his accountant. He walked toward the vestibule and lowered his voice. "Prav's family. Cut the support."

"What?" asked the confused accountant.

"You heard me."

"But they have rent due—and all those medical bills, food, and..."

Hyde boiled over as he listened to the list of shit he covered for his ungrateful, ignorant, foreign-born in-laws. He was sick of them all. "Nothing. Let them beg for it."

Hyde ended the call and smirked with satisfaction, enjoying his play as he got in his private elevator. A grin lit his face while preparing to greet any onlookers in his exquisite lobby, but when the gold doors slid open, a smelly gaggle of immigrants from the cleaning service marred his view. *Goddamn it. They're supposed to use the employee elevators.* He shot them a warning glare and made a mental note to fire the manager of the service. Hiring illegal immigrants was a cost-effective strategy, but for God's sake, Hyde didn't want to look at them.

Later, not long after the Macchi cop was attacked, Hyde made good on his studio visit and strolled through the front door. He perked up at his excellent timing when he spotted Alex glaring at him across the room. Hyde walked over to a small group of people within Alex's earshot and, without preamble, interjected himself into the conversation.

"So hey, did I tell ya, the mayor, personal friend of mine—Pravdina and I were having dinner with him and his wife, although, wow, she hasn't aged well, am I right? Anyway, we were talking about the crime rates in the city, and this off-duty cop who got mugged down in Bay Ridge. Did you hear about it? Unfortunate, really, but then again, cops—some of them can't be trusted either."

Hyde threw his hands in the air and made sure Alex was listening. "I mean, it's a very dangerous neighborhood, very dangerous, but I heard the cop was doing a drug deal or something. It just goes to show you, you can never tell. You gotta watch your back. You better watch your back. When you're in a dirty business, you never know when the hammer's gonna fall on you. A dirty cop is what I heard. Maybe he had it coming."

Hyde smirked as Alex Macchi walked out of the studio. "Putz," he said, under his breath.

ALEX HAD WITNESSED the confused looks on the faces of Hyde's audience, but avoided making eye contact with the man himself while he carried on. It took every ounce of control Alex could muster to turn from the room and walk outside. His gut in a knot, his fist clenched, he yanked open the door on his waiting car. Renzo was in the driver's seat.

He got inside and slammed the door. "Shit!" Alex yelled.

Renzo unbuckled his seat belt and put his hand on the door. "What happened?"

When Alex told him about Hyde's rant that was directed at him, Renzo ground his teeth and shook his head. "That prick. You want me to go knock the shit out of him? Just say the word. Be my pleasure."

"No, but thanks for the thought. Go inside and wait for Petunia. I can't look at him." Renzo gave him a hard look and got out of the car.

Alex pulled out his phone and called his brother. "Michael, you still at the office?" Alex's brow creased with concern as he watched Renzo, looming large in his always-present jacket concealing a handgun, pat it as he walked into the dance studio.

"What's wrong?" said Michael.

"Ah, hell, it's Hyde. Listen, we need to talk. Can you meet me at the apartment? I should be there in about thirty minutes."

"No problem."

Once home and after Michael arrived, they told Petunia they needed to speak privately. She was more than happy to take a plate of food into her room. Lily was asleep as Alex, Charlotte, and Michael went into the office and slid closed the soundproof glass doors. They sat facing one another over a glass-topped coffee table as Alex gave them the latest on Hyde's antics.

"He's taunting us, Alex," Charlotte crossed her arms. "He's trying to get you to come after him. He *wants* you to lose control."

"I know, but it's more than that. This proves he's aware of what's happening in Bay Ridge. He owns the place; he's got some connection or business going on at the warehouse. He pays the taxes on it. His holding company, Mercer Investment Group, owns it, so he's involved."

Michael nodded. "He knew exactly what he was doing. Charlotte is right, though, he was taunting you. You can't let him sucker you into some kind of physical altercation."

Alex's eyes got large as he pounded on the arms of the chair. "Dammit! He assaulted my wife, and Tony could have been killed because he was looking into this asshole for us. I'm holding Hyde responsible."

Charlotte and Michael glanced at each other as Alex took a deep breath and continued. "I think we go to the cops and tell them we think something illegal's happening at that warehouse. See if they can be pressured to check into it. Santa and Josh have been watching from their perch, keeping a journal, and cars and trucks are in and out of there all the time. Vans too. It's got to be some type of distribution warehouse. Maybe drugs. Most of the stuff is loaded or unloaded around the back, so we can't get a good look at that. We haven't seen them use the pier, but maybe we could make something up, find a reason to get an inspector in there."

Michael leaned forward, his arms resting on his knees. "We have the license plates of most of the vehicles coming and going. Several of them belong to a company called Med Source. They supply or ship textiles, electronics, medical equipment; we're not sure what else. Bacon's looking into Med Source as we speak, but I'm not sure the cops would have reason to search the compound without a warrant. They damn sure aren't going to spend the kind of time and money we are just watching the place. Before we go to the cops, we need something solid that they would be interested in."

"Well, I'm more convinced than ever that Hyde's dirty, and he obviously knows Tony's my brother," said Alex as he gripped his fist in the air. "He knew what he was saying about him, which means he knows it was my brother on his property. I'm going to call Baach and tell them that we need to take the contractors' action nationwide." Alex's anger grew. "We open it up to *any* project in the States, not just in the city, that Hyde has worked on. I'll bet he's screwed over hundreds of people. Maybe it could even be a class action. Let's take out ads in the trade papers, go to the unions, and let *everyone* know that if they've ever had a beef with Hyde, we're interested."

"Baach is going to need to hire a team of lawyers to keep up with this much work. And you know some crazies will come out only to waste our time," Charlotte cautioned.

He glared at her. "I know."

"And you know that if we do that, Hyde will become even more outraged with us than he is right now."

"Yes, I know that, Charlotte," Alex challenged.

Charlotte clasped her hands and softened her voice. "He's going to try to take it out on all of us, and he'll bring his hatred into the studio and to the girls. He already did that by assaulting me there and talking trash about Tony in front of you."

"I realize that." Alex blinked, glancing briefly at the concern on Michael's face.

Charlotte's face flushed as she looked at him. "If we're going public, Alex, then it's time we have a further talk with Petunia, so she'll be prepared. Simone is her father's daughter. She lights up whenever he's around, so I suspect she'll be angry with us, as well, about publicly shaming him. She'll use her team of groupies, and I guarantee this will blow back on Petunia and her friends. The studio will not like it, either, when they get wind of it."

Alex sat back and threw his hands up. "I'm sure they've had parents in competing industries or who've been in bed together over a bad deal. This isn't really any of their business."

Charlotte nodded. "No, I'm sure you're right, but I'm not sure I've heard of anyone *publishing it* in the newspapers before. If we go that far, and I'm not saying we shouldn't, it's going to bounce back on us. I just want us to think about it before we move forward."

Alex swallowed hard as he continued to press. "I get what you're saying, Charlotte. I do. But the season is practically over, and the girls don't go to the same school. I think the problems with Simone and Hyde will surface next year and not in the next couple weeks. That shouldn't matter anyway. Hyde's dirty. He assaulted you, and he nearly killed Tony. No way I can let this go. This is my campaign."

Charlotte crossed her legs and arms. "I understand, Alex. I'm just as angry with Hyde as you are, but I want us to move carefully. Maybe I should speak with Jill at the studio and see what she has to say. Let me give her a call to see if she can meet, and after that we'll break the news to Petunia."

Alex stretched his neck, thinking through the fallout for his daughter. He and Charlotte stared at one another until Alex closed his eyes with resignation and rubbed his head. "If you think this is going to get too big for Petunia, if you don't think she can handle it, we can back off. I get it. We'll just follow through with the commitments we've already made and shut the rest of this thing down. I know she's been through enough over the past couple of years. You know I'd never hurt her."

"Alex, please stop," Charlotte said, taking his hand. "I know you'd never hurt her. It's just that a part of me thinks you're coming at this to protect our honor, having a duel with someone who did something to your woman and your brother."

She reached up and laid a soft hand on his face. "I just want us to be clear about the reasons we're taking these steps. I don't ever want us to be at odds or let these things come between us. So, yes, if Petunia is horrifically upset about the possibility of leaving the studio, which has been her second home for the last four years, and if leaving is going to set her back or make her truly unhappy, then we need to find another way...or discuss it as a family. In the end, *our family, the Macchi family, our children*, are *all* that's important. So let's tell Bacon to keep digging and look closer at Med Source. I'll have a quiet word with Jill, and then we'll see where we're at."

Michael said, "It's a good plan, Alex. We keep digging, but we keep it quiet. As usual, we don't want 'em to see us coming."

Alex threw his head back and took in a deep breath through his nose. "All right. Let's sleep on it and see where we are tomorrow."

Charlotte glanced at Michael and then Alex. "I'm sorry he said those things about Tony, but Hyde Sutton is just a classic bully. He's pushing you to see if you push back, and if you do, he'll push back harder and play dirty. He's a bad guy, and you're a wonderful guy, so just remember that you've already won, honey."

Alex looked into his wife's warm eyes and gave her a half smile. "Thank you, Charlotte. I appreciate it."

"You're very welcome."

Chapter 12

CHARLOTTE MET WITH Jill Farrell at a coffee shop near the studio the next afternoon. Jill had been in the dance world all of her life and was a graceful, effective, and fair-minded business owner who could be counted on for her discretion. One thing Alex had gotten right the night before was that it was a small world, and Jill wouldn't be able to keep her doors open if she ever angered the wrong person or took sides in the dancers' daily mini-dramas. She was a cool customer, and Charlotte was confident that their conversation would never get back to Hyde or his family.

Jill spoke briefly about her excitement over summer classes, and Charlotte realized she had to get to the point. She brought Jill up to speed on the legal situation between themselves and Hyde.

Jill raised an eyebrow and took a sip of her cappuccino. "Yes, I heard something about that."

Charlotte toyed with her cup and tilted her head. "We want to force Hyde to play fair and pick on someone his own size. As you can imagine, this has irritated the man."

Jill looked at her under hooded brows. "I imagine it did."

Charlotte assessed Jill. Still believing she could trust her, she took a deep breath and continued, "But the other day, at the studio, after the committee meeting, Hyde cornered me in the conference room and sexually assaulted me. He grabbed me and made an insulting comment."

Jill's jaw dropped. Her hand flew out and grabbed Charlotte's arm. "My God! That's horrible. I'm so sorry!"

Charlotte looked down. "It was horrible, but I didn't want to create a scene in front of the girls, so I just left. Hyde probably thinks he got away with it. Alex, as you can imagine, was furious." She went on to explain about Hyde's further provocation of Alex the day before.

"That's terrible," Jill said, her hand on her heart.

Charlotte nodded. "He's a bully, and I wanted you to know that he's bringing it into the studio. I know you won't repeat this to anyone else, but I thought you needed to know that things have gotten ugly. In fact, we're thinking about turning up the heat on him further, and we know now he won't take it lying down. Hyde'll retaliate against us, and I believe he'll drag Simone into the mix, if he hasn't already."

Jill closed her eyes briefly and shook her head. "What can I do to help you, Charlotte? Are you pressing charges against Hyde?"

"No, not at this time, but we were wondering what your reaction would be because we're going to speak with Petunia tonight and wanted to lay out our options."

Jill gave her a soft, appreciative look. "I understand, and you want my thoughts? Okay. Just so you know, you're right, I promise I won't repeat anything about our conversation with anyone else. But if Petunia leaves the studio over this, I'll be very sad, not only for her but for the other girls. She's a natural leader, Charlotte. She keeps them steady and has just the right amount of empathy for their problems, but she knows when enough is enough and it's time to face your problems and get back to work. And that's just her character. She's a strong dancer, and her team would miss her too. She's become a standout, and we're all really proud of the hard work she puts into practice."

Jill took a deep breath and leaned forward. "That aside, I can't tell you how much I loathe Hyde Sutton. I rarely tell other parents how I feel about anyone, but now that I know what he did to you, in my studio, I want him gone. I never want to see his putrid face again. I understand if you want to bring the police into this, but I'm going to counsel you against it. It will be your word against his, and while a business conflict is one thing, a charge of sexually assaulting someone is completely another."

Charlotte looked away because she knew that although she wasn't planning to report the assault, she and Alex had their own plans of retaliation that she couldn't share. But a day hadn't gone by in which her thoughts weren't conflicted. "Doesn't that make me a coward? A terrible role model? Shouldn't I speak up no matter the consequences? Wouldn't that be the right thing to do?"

"Not a coward, Charlotte." Jill frowned. "A realist. You may hate me for it, but this isn't the first report I've gotten about Hyde. Over the years, you're actually the third woman to tell me that he made unwanted sexual advances, but you're the first one where it's happened at my school. I believed them, and I believe you, and I didn't know how to advise them at the time because maybe I was thinking more about my studio than I was about the mothers who were assaulted. I just wanted it to go away! My life's work is in that place. I've put my sweat and blood, literally, into it and have an envied, successful dance studio in Manhattan. We're a sister studio with Julliard and, as you know, we have a tremendous relationship with the New York City Ballet. I built that, and I was just too afraid that a scandal would make my school distasteful by association for some of the families who send their children here."

Jill sat back and wiped a small tear of frustration that appeared in the corner of her eye. "And how in the world can I get rid of the Sutton family? On what grounds? But you know what I tell myself? In the long run, I think I've better served the greater good by giving the children a positive, safe place to grow, develop their skills, and become strong girls and women. I sometimes feel like I've had a real hand in helping an army of kids find their inner strength through this sport, and I'm proud of that. If I'd chosen differently, or counseled the other women differently, who knows? Maybe I'd still be here, maybe I wouldn't. So we all have to make choices and whatever choice you make, I'll support you in any way I can. No matter what you decide. Hyde Sutton is a pig. A bad man. But screw him. I really believe he'll get his one day and, in the meantime, I want to teach my students to be strong and ready for the world when challenges are thrown at them."

Charlotte relaxed her intertwined hands which had clenched upon hearing the reports. "It's hard to hear that he's been doing this to other women, but I'm not surprised, and I understand why you wanted to protect yourself and the studio. Women...." She exhaled loudly before she continued, "So many of us are faced with this stuff all of our lives. I'm fairly confident, at least at this point, that I'm not going to the police. God knows that Petunia and I don't need the attention. I don't want to tell Petunia about the assault. Not yet anyway. She's had to grow up so fast, and this would be just another blow to her innocence. She'd probably feel like she'd need to come to my aid because another horrid adult did something bad. I want her to be safe, and that hasn't been easy. But the reality is there's bad blood now between us and Hyde, and Petunia needs to be aware of it in case there's a backlash."

The two women absorbed the situation and Charlotte asked, "What do you think Simone will do?"

Jill shook her head slowly. "From what I've observed, I think Simone Sutton is sadly being groomed in her father's playbook. She worships him, and he nurtures that all the time. Have you ever listened to how he speaks to her? Speaks *about* her? It's inappropriate and upsetting, but I don't know what to do. I worry about Simone, I do. But basically, it's none of my business how people raise their children unless I suspect something evil—which I don't."

Jill sighed. "But I think I can predict that Simone will completely stand by her father. Always. And sixth graders? Simone has a real grasp about how to run a hive. Her family's name, their wealth, their image...it's heady stuff for some of the folks who love to have bragging rights. She knows this. She's not a bad kid, but I see a pattern of parenting, which is troubling, and I've sadly seen too many of the wealthy kids make some very poor decisions. I hope Simone finds her strength of character in time, and I hope she doesn't try to hurt your daughter along the way. I don't know if this is helpful or not, but it's all I've got."

Charlotte nodded. "Thanks for your support, Jill. If you don't mind, would you let me know if you hear anything?"

"That I can do. At least in the studio, I have some power. If the girls decide to act badly, I will call them out on it. Thank you for trusting me, and I'll do what I can to maintain the peace."

"I'll let you know what we decide to do." Charlotte reached for her bag intending to leave.

"Listen," Jill said, reaching out, "I think you and Alex should feel good about standing up to Hyde on behalf of the little guy. It's just another reason I don't want you to be run off. I'm proud to have you and your family in my life."

Charlotte gave her a small smile. "Thanks, Jill. We'll see."

Chapter 13

Across town, Viktor Timofeyev sat next to a large, empty banquet table dressed for a reception later that night. Always on the move and worried about being overheard, he conducted his nomadic business on burner phones and in different environments owned by friendly associates. His long legs splayed wide, he reached toward the table, picked up a bottle of vodka, and poured a drink while he listened intently to the report. Not offering his men a chair, they stood at attention in front of him.

"Andy didn't know he was a cop. After he took him down, he went through his pockets and saw the badge and decided he shouldn't kill him because it might attract even more attention. So they got him out of there and threw him in the weeds outside. The cop couldn't have seen anything because it was a quiet day, no shipments, and you can't see in the windows, so yeah, that's all I know."

Viktor put his empty glass down, then stretched his long arms, clasping his hands behind his head. He had a small army of soldiers handling his day-to-day operations. He'd learned to protect himself from his illegal activities. It was their job to do the dirty work, while he enjoyed the profits. But there could never, ever be any mistake about who was in charge.

Viktor considered his soldier with the long scar down one side of his face. "Why do you think cop, detective, was inside property?"

The man swallowed hard. "He was snooping, looking around."

"Yes. Why would he do that? Do you think we have leak? Is someone talking? Has someone been arrested and turning tail on us?"

The man with the scar shook his head. "I don't think so, Viktor. I don't. Could be, I suppose, but I haven't heard anything."

Viktor threw out his long, long arms. "So why? Has to be why. Put on thinking caps for this."

The two men squirmed under his glare but kept silent.

"So you think of nothing? Maybe we increase security. Get dogs?"

The two men shuffled their feet until the other soldier said, "You wanted the place to look casual and not over protected. If we bring in a bunch of security shit, and dogs, it'll look like we're trying to hide something. But you said we should 'hide in plain sight'—that it was smarter."

"It is smarter. For now. But now we have cop. *Alive* cop."

"You think we should have killed him?"

Viktor slowly stroked his mustache. "No. You were right. It was good decision. No one is asleep at wheel? Another harbor event, fireworks off Liberty Island will coincide with our delivery, and I want no problems."

"No problems, boss. We'll be ready. Just like always. The women walk the plank dressed like stoned party girls and get into the vans. As long as the transfer at sea onto the party boat goes off again, it's the perfect cover with all the fireworks and the pleasure-boat activity in the harbor."

Viktor smiled, proudly displaying his crooked, yellow teeth. He looked down at his bejeweled gold watch and checked the time. He got up and reached his arms forward, placing a firm hand on each of the two soldiers faces. "Remember, you take good care of these women. I don't care if you try them out once they get to warehouse, but no rough stuff, no spread of disease. We make quarter million from each one, so remind everyone to treat them like priceless racing horse. They can't be rode too hard or value goes away."

His comrade with the cruel scar smiled.

Viktor knew when to give bonus on job.

Chapter 14

OVER SECURE LINES in the room at the Macchi & Macchi headquarters, Bacon once more delivered the requested information. Michael, Alex, and Charlotte listened and made notes as he went over the findings.

"So Med Source, it's all in my e-mail to you, man. It's a subsidiary of a shell company named ZATO, which is registered in Delaware, probably because it's protected by the Delaware Business Judgment Rule, which has some cool shields. No owner name listed on it; set up by a law firm, so whoever set it up gets attorney-client privilege. ZATO has some other subsidiaries, some LLCs; don't know what they do, but I'm thinking if they're layering up, then ZATO's got some other layer subsidiaries elsewhere, like offshore, probably in Panama City, if I were them."

Bacon drew a deep breath. "So what you're going to find about them, or what the *IRS or the law* could find out about ZATO would be crap. You'd need court orders to get more. But as we know, I'm not the law, so I wormed around—on your dime, kids—and I got a name.

"Med Source does some purchasing and distribution of medical supplies, mostly, and some other shit, so it's got a few real employees. But Med Source is just a big baby, and you always wanna look for the mama. What you want to know is who started it, or who runs it, or the organization of the shell: what and where all those subs are, and what the hell they do. But hey, that could take a while, so I stopped when I got a *name* that might mean something: Viktor Timofeyev. Stupid Delaware lawyer had it in a file on ZATO paperwork. This would have been years ago, man, so he probably forgot it was even there. Viktor's name is not listed in the public records, of course, but it was there in the files I snatched up—and I figured if the lawyer was stupid enough to put it in there, then it had to be legit."

Bacon loudly crunched on something for a while before he continued, "So, I did some digging into Viktor Timofeyev. Dude! Awesome shit, but you're not going to like it. Guy's like a Russian legend. Immigrated from St. Petersburg, years ago, got his fucking green card, man, and set up shop. He's what you might call an actual Russian mob boss, folks. No shit. He's not a man to mess with. There's a fucking picture of him in Russia when he was some super athlete like in that *Rocky* movie or something. Anyway, he has a son, Roman Timofeyev, who has his green card too. Roman graduated from NYU and works in real estate. In fact, Roman's the dude who owns Med Source."

"So Hyde Sutton has a warehouse in Bay Ridge with a pier, and he's letting the Russian mafia use it?" asked Alex.

"If a ZATO subsidiary has some operation over there in Bay Ridge, then I think the dots connect back to Viktor, whose alias, by the way, is '*the fucking Arm.*' Well, not the *fucking* arm, I threw in the F word to highlight the coolness of his nickname. From the picture I unearthed, the man has some pretty cool ink, and if I get a spare minute, I'm gonna see if I can't rez it up and transcribe what the hell his tats say. I'll keep you posted. What else you want from me?"

"Hang on," said Charlotte, "I've heard of Roman Timofeyev. Alex, he was a benefactor at last year's Red Cross ball. I don't think we met him, but I remember the name."

Alex looked at the phone. "Bacon, find out what you can about *Roman* Timofeyev. Specifically, see if he has any business with Hyde Sutton. Look into their charity circles and other businesses—legitimate or not. I need to see where the Timofeyevs—who are using the warehouse complex—and Hyde Sutton, its owner, cross paths. I've got to assume they do, otherwise why would Hyde let them use it? Hyde's not reporting any income from the property. That's right, isn't it, Bacon?"

"I don't see it, not through Med Source anyway."

Michael had moved to the white board and was making notes. He drew lines and added some names.

Alex said, "Technically, Mercer Investments owns it, but Hyde owns Mercer, so could Med Source be paying Hyde directly? Look into that, too, but focus on Roman for now. He's out there, running in the New York social set, so maybe that's how he met Hyde."

Alex screwed up his face as a noise came over the phone: the slurping from a straw when it reached the bottom of a cup.

"I'm on it," said Bacon, "but I'm putting you on notice that my fees will *greatly* increase if I find too many firewalls with your new Russian mob friends. I don't usually give a shit, but have you seen that movie with Viggo Mortensen, you know, the dude from the *Lord of the Rings* movies? He plays a badass Russian in this movie *Eastern Promises*, and I don't want to get mixed up with that shit."

"Thank you for the warning." Alex rolled his eyes. "Do what you can. We appreciate it."

Bacon disconnected and they looked at each other, wondering where things were headed now.

Chapter 15

SANTIAGO, OR SANTA—as he was known by his associates at Macchi & Macchi—was kicked back in the shadows of the empty office space across from the Bay Ridge Properties complex, enjoying the late-June fireworks display over New York Bay. Slightly bored from the tedium that often came with surveillance jobs and the inactivity that usually persisted over the course of his evening shift watching the complex, he was surprised to see a large boat, heading north from the Narrows, that appeared to be approaching the pier at the back of the warehouse.

Santa jumped up and positioned the cameras to zoom in and videotape the event and pulled up his field binoculars for a closer look. Never really able to get a good look at the back of the property from his vantage, they did have partial viewing access to the pier and dock as it protruded past the line of the buildings into the harbor.

His suspicions were confirmed that the boat was headed toward the complex pier when several men emerged from the warehouse and walked down to the dock to help secure the boat's tie lines. With very little preamble, it docked, and Santa was confused as he watched roughly ten to twelve women—all in various states of dishevelment and sparkly dress—stagger off the boat. They were roughly directed by the men from the warehouse to get into the back of two waiting vans. The boat immediately pulled away from the pier and continued north into the harbor. The loaded vans drove through the complex and left through the front gates, heading north. After that, all the lights in the place went dim, and the party was over.

Unsure of what he'd seen, Santa downloaded the video and sent it to Alex and Michael. Reviewing it after he'd hit Send, he got a better look at the women's faces, and what he saw alarmed him. They didn't look healthy. From a distance, they appeared to be a bunch of party girls, but up close, they sure as shit were not having a good time. Several of them were crying, and one face, in particular, that Santa froze on was filled with obvious trauma or fear. Wherever these women came from, and wherever they went, they sure as shit didn't want to be there. Santa grabbed his phone and texted Alex: *Just sent a video. Urgent. This is bad.*

THE NEXT MORNING, Alex and Charlotte arrived at the midtown office building of Macchi & Macchi and somberly rode up in the elevator to the sixth floor. The firm offices were some of the most tightly secured places in Manhattan. Designed specifically to protect the employees, customers, and their work from all prying eyes and ears, the high-ceilinged loft space was broken into public spaces and private. The private spaces contained priceless and illegally obtained materials and equipment. Soundproof and bug-proof, the entire office was a security fiefdom filled with highly advanced technology and muscle for any job on the planet.

Alex pressed a code into the outer door of the Mr. Hyde war room, and the two entered. He flipped on the lights, revealing a masterpiece of detailed organization put together with expert patience by Karla Fernandez. Every report from Bacon; the players from the contractor disputes; and every piece of private information obtained about Hyde Sutton, his business empires, and his personal life were displayed around the room in a comprehensive manner.

Michael and Karla joined them around the conference table, and the four watched the video again together.

Alex, grim-faced, asked, "So what do we see? What's happening in this video?"

Karla, a short, highly energetic former Marine, who had joined the company after leaving the military said, "I don't have all the answers, but I can tell you that I've seen that same look before, and it's terror. Shock. Distress. They weren't clean. Something bad happened to them and is probably still happening as we speak. They were not on that dock or put into those vans voluntarily, which means they were captives. They were certainly not there to have fun, which means that they were being hurt. Used. And women are typically used for sex, so my guess would be that they were either prostitutes back from some traumatic, dismal excursion, or they're captives, literally. Not girls for hire released back onto the streets after a night of work. Since they were deposited in the dark and hurtled into the back of a couple of paneled vans, my guess is that they're captives."

"Human trafficking?" said Charlotte. "I can't believe this is happening. Are we really sitting on evidence that the warehouse is tied to human trafficking? That Hyde Sutton is involved in sex trafficking?"

"I think we are," said Alex. "It's the only logical conclusion, and Karla's right. Those women looked bad. I've not witnessed what she has, but I think we should believe her. Michael, what's your opinion?"

Michael nodded. "I agree, and now that I see this, I regret we didn't have the manpower in place to follow the vans. Santa thought they looked like the vans he'd seen around there before, but when we ran the plates, they showed up as for-sale vehicles from a Brooklyn used car lot. No telling where the vans took the girls, but I've got one of our guys over at the sales lot in Brooklyn this morning checking to see if these vans, with the plates Santa got, are in the lot. If they are, then I've got to believe that they dumped the women somewhere and returned the vans. If they only 'borrowed' the vans, they must have an arrangement with the owner. We'll need to chase this down."

Karla was at the white board frantically making notes.

Alex continued, "So we need to have someone on the street, or stashed down the street, ready to head out on a moment's notice to follow the vans if we see another shipment. We need to find out where they're being taken. If we're right, then the women they transferred last night are in danger, and we need to take this to the police."

Michael swiveled in his chair, his arms folded and his head on his chest. He raised his eyes and said, "We need to be clear about what our goals are, Alex. This operation was to find out just how dirty Hyde Sutton is and to see where we could hurt him. If he's tied to human trafficking, then I agree we need to go to the cops. But, as I see it, the Bay Ridge compound's being used by the Russian mafia."

Michael went over to the white board and stood next to pictures they'd obtained of Viktor and Roman Timofeyev. "It's probably a miracle that Tony got out of there with his life. The Russians are protecting the place, and now we think we know why. We don't know what else they might be moving in and out, but that's the first boat that's we've seen. Before we risk the lives of our employees, Alex, we need to figure out who we're up against, and if it's the Russian mob, that changes things."

Michael pointed to the names on the board. "This is too big for us now; it's not who we are and what we do. The cops are going to be interested, but I don't know how long it will take for them to mobilize. So I agree that, for the time being, we continue the surveillance, but Santa and Josh and now a third guy have gotta be really careful over there and watch their backs. If the Russian mob finds out we're spying on them, they'll kill us, Alex, make no mistake about it."

The group was silent, staring at the board as Michael sat back in his chair. Karla walked to a picture of Hyde Sutton and pointed at it. "So let's talk about Hyde. He's the man we've been chasing, and last night Bacon sent another report over about Roman Timofeyev and his real estate development company. Yet another one for the war board." She pointed to the new entry and said: "International Development Partners. You asked Bacon to find a link between the Timofeyevs and Hyde Sutton, and he found a couple.

"Roman and Mr. Hyde have a hotel and convention center development deal in St. Petersburg, Russia. There's another one on the books for Prague, but it looks like they've already broken ground in St. Petersburg. In addition, Mercer Investment Group, the owner of Bay Ridge Properties, has several investors. One of them is Roman Timofeyev. So yeah, if we're looking for a connection, there it is. Should have seen that one, but we were focusing on Med Source and then stumbled onto ZATO. I mean, shit, the Timofeyev name alone brings you straight to the mob."

"So Hyde's in bed with these guys," Alex stated, his jaw working, tense.

"Definitely," said Karla.

Alex rocked in his chair. "To summarize: Hyde Sutton is a partner with Roman Timofeyev in an investment group, and he's working on real estate deals in Russia and the Czech Republic with the Russian mafia. He owns a warehouse that just *happens* to have a pier in New York Harbor, and he's letting the Russians use it for human trafficking. Unbelievable. He just turned over the keys to a valuable port of entry to the Russian mafia, and he either knew what they were using it for or looked the other way. Either way, he's guilty and must be held accountable."

"What if he didn't know about the human trafficking," Michael offered. "Can we really get him to take the fall for this? Would the cops even be able to charge him? The man will lawyer up so fast, it might not happen. I guarantee he would scream his innocence."

"Look at the faces of those women," said Charlotte. "We have pictures and video that we must bring to the police so they can find them. This needs to stop! Making Hyde accountable is one thing, but we need to help *them*. We can't turn our backs on this. Jesus, it makes me sick. Even if Hyde doesn't know everything about what's going on, he's financing the operation by giving them a shop to run it from. He's got money tied up with them."

Karla shrugged. "Driver of the car is as guilty as the ones who commit the crime."

Charlotte pointed angrily toward the video. "They're making money off the backs of innocent women and using that money to do a real estate deal with Hyde Sutton. Hyde is guilty, and he's sick! You're right, Michael, we do need to be clear about what Macchi & Macchi is going to do, so let me tell you. We're going to get the cops involved. Today. They *will be* interested, and we'll need to work with them.

"We'll offer them our assistance to shut this thing down and find the women. And you're right about Hyde lawyering up. He's got all kinds of layers between him and the Russian mob, and they probably won't be able to touch him. Everyone's so afraid of slander and his stinking lawsuits; they know Hyde and his lawyers will threaten the life out of the DA's office if they defame him without cause. So, we need to inflict some pain on Hyde Sutton and tie him to the operation, then we're going to put a goddamned bow on it and hand him over to the cops."

Alex knew there was another evil layer to Hyde's sins, and his wife was losing patience. They all were.

Karla clicked her tongue. "Okay then. We're going to need more information, the kind that Bacon can't uncover. Real live conversations between Hyde and the Russians. We need to get a bug or two into his home, his computer, his phone, his car—basically, anywhere he goes. We need to get inside."

They looked at one another, thinking. "We could see if there are any rentals in the building on a floor close to his penthouse and get an interceptor with an antenna to help pick up the conversations," suggested Alex.

"But how can we plant the mics and cameras in Hyde's apartment?" said Karla, walking over to the board with Hyde's personal information. She scanned it and pointed to the options. "The only ones who live with him are his wife and kid and a twenty-five-year old maid named Bijoux. She came into the country from France as their au pair. The rest of their staff are service providers from agencies."

They stared at a picture of a young woman with a sweet,

beautiful smile and long dark braided hair from her listing with the international au pair agency.

"Who do we know would be able to successfully convince this lovely, young French immigrant to spy on her employer?" said Alex, looking knowingly at Michael.

A side of Michael's mouth turned up. "He's on hiatus with his family in Hawaii."

"Get him off the surfboard and on the next plane out. Owen is perfect for the job. I want him here tomorrow."

"He does have a way about him," Karla smiled, too.

"All right," said Alex. "I'll divert Bacon into finding everything he can about Hyde's maid, Bijoux Demey. We need to find her weaknesses and then send in the lovable, female-captivating Owen Kai to convince her to help us. I'll check on an available real estate rental in Sutton Tower to see if we can get a place close enough to pick up a signal to record from Hyde's apartment. Michael, round up the cops and get them up to speed, and let our guys know what they're up against."

Charlotte said, "I'm going to do some research on my own with some victim aid organizations and see what happens to these women if they're ever found."

"Do you think it's time to bring your family up to speed?" asked Alex.

Charlotte nodded. "I'll give them a call. They're not going to like it... or maybe they will. I know they'll think it's too dangerous, but I'm sure they won't fault the cause. We need to be careful, all of us, but we need to find those women. They're suffering, and we might be the only ones who have a thread of knowledge about where they are."

They broke up the meeting and got to work.

JULY

Chapter 16

Bijoux Demey hated her job with the Sutton family. To be fair, she really only hated Hyde Sutton, but the entire place stank of the man. Not literally, of course, but everywhere she looked were the constant reminders that she lived and worked in the same space as him. His stamp was on everything from the furniture, walls, ceilings, moldings, and gaudy gold fixtures—all the way down to the women living with him. He dressed the three of them to fit in with his fantasy life, and it disgusted her.

When she'd received a call from the au pair service that a family in the United States had viewed her profile and wanted to set up an interview via Skype, she was encouraged that she might actually secure a position there. While she was nervous about the possibility of moving to America, it would be a chance to grow as a person and see what another country might offer and to leave behind the stagnant and hopeless situation of her home in France.

Bijoux, then all of twenty-three, was the middle of five children born to a working-class family. The cramped conditions in their small home were sometimes unbearable, but the worst part was that she regretted not studying harder in school. With the exception of learning English, which came easily to her for some reason, the only other skill she possessed was culinary. She'd learned to cook from her father, who was a chef, but not one who made much money because he beleaguered his family to contribute to their household income in order to survive. Pressed into the role of cooking the family meals, Bijoux always had very little money or energy to invest in her future. She had dreams, but even though she was only twenty-three, she was depressed that her reality didn't include them.

The au pair service had told her a little about how to prepare for the Skype family interview, and Bijoux assumed that it would be conducted by the mother. She was surprised when her first discussion took place with the father and daughter, Hyde and Simone Sutton. Mr. Sutton had explained that he wanted his daughter to have daily exposure to the French language, since he felt it important for her to have that support since she was studying it in school. They were an active, busy family, he insisted, so even though there was only one child in the household, they could always use the help.

It seemed a bit untraditional for an older child to require an au pair, but the agency said they were legit. When Bijoux saw the opportunity to move to New York City, she took it. After arriving in America, she was stunned to realize that the family was super rich. In her wildest dreams she could never have envisioned herself living in a millionaire's penthouse overlooking Manhattan.

But the unfortunate tradeoff was Hyde Sutton. She soon realized he was going to be a problem. He hovered around her and sometimes invaded her personal space, making her uncomfortable. She never encouraged Mr. Sutton and was careful to avoid him whenever possible, but he continued to linger and had recently become even more obnoxious and vulgar than usual. Mr. Sutton was too interested in her and made his intentions clear in inappropriate and offensive ways.

Bijoux also came to realize that the mother, Pravdina, was not overly supportive of her presence in the home, and her supposed charge, Simone, was ambivalent as well. After speaking with Pravdina about her duties, or the lack thereof, when Simone was not around, they came to a mutual agreement that she would be in charge of the meals once they discovered she was an excellent cook. In short order, Simone completely lost interest in spending time with Bijoux and since Simone was not encouraged to do so by her parents, they informally transferred Bijoux's duties to full-time cook. And Mr. Sutton bought her a uniform. And not even a cook's uniform, but a throwback to a blousy French maid. It was ridiculous, and they all knew it, but Bijoux's choice was to wear it or return to France.

While deeply unhappy that her situation had turned out to be so uncomfortable, she was determined to make the best of her circumstances while allowed to stay in the United States. In fact, the Sutton family had just completed an extension of her visa. Neither party had informed the au pair agency or the government that she was now functioning as a cook. Once this visa expired in about eight months, she would have to return to France—unless a miracle came along to become a full-time student and she could transfer her status. Fat chance. Even if she saved every penny she made, which was nearly impossible once her family found out about her circumstances, she would never have enough money to support herself as a full-time student in the United States.

Bijoux felt certain that Pravdina was not interested in helping her, and there was no way she would go to Hyde Sutton for a favor. She knew that was exactly the opportunity he was waiting for—so she could express her gratitude by God-only-knows what terms.

What she did do, however, was enroll in Saturday classes at the Culinary Institute of America (CIA) and hoped for the best. There she discovered that even though cooking had been a forced labor for her at home in France, it was different in New York, and she loved it; plus she was good at it. While staying at the Suttons' she had the rare privilege of an unlimited shopping budget and could purchase any exotic and expensive ingredients she wanted to experiment with. As long as dinner was served on time and tasted pretty good, none of the Suttons really cared.

That Saturday, as Bijoux entered her class at the CIA in Hyde Park to work on her sauces, she was lost in thought about the decisions she would be forced to make in the coming months. Taking her usual seat for the instructional portion of the class, she was surprised when a man she had never seen before asked if the seat beside her was taken. Indicating it wasn't, the man gave her the most endearing smile and said, "*Merci.*"

Bijoux was startled by the French word and naturally asked him if he spoke French. "I suppose that's my presumption?" she said.

"No," he laughed. "I don't really speak French, just a few words. Maybe it's a hangover from the French cooking classes."

"Ah. Are you new here? I don't remember seeing you in class before."

"Yes. I am. My name's Owen. I just moved here from California."

"Oh! My name's Bijoux."

"*Enchanté,*" Owen smiled, tossing his hair. "Are you from France?"

Bijoux blushed at the French greeting and how he delivered it. Owen was adorable. A little older, maybe thirty, he had longish dark hair, a healthy tan, and looked like someone who spent a lot of time outdoors and not in a kitchen. Deeply set brown eyes and a smile, which revealed a perfect set of white teeth, and large dimples, he seemed as if he didn't have a care in the world.

It had been an extremely long time since Bijoux had dated anyone, and this man was terribly good-looking. As the cooking portion of the class got underway, Owen asked to share a station with her, and they had more fun than she knew was possible while learning about the techniques for making *béchamel.*

Her new cooking companion was one of the nicest men she had met since arriving in America, and by the end of the class she desperately hoped they could continue their friendship. Owen did not disappoint, asking if she would meet him the next day for a walk in Central Park. She jumped at the invitation.

Regrettably, leaving behind the gorgeous man and his intoxicating attention, she caught the train back to Manhattan. Once out of his reach, she realized she didn't know much about him, other than he, oddly, didn't seem too adept in the kitchen. But she also realized she didn't care. With an excitement she hadn't felt in a long time, her mind flew to the options in her limited wardrobe and what she should wear for her first real date with him. *Golly! I don't even know his last name.*

Chapter 17

THE NEXT DAY, after receiving a text from Owen about where to meet, Bijoux walked to the park at a fast pace, eager to discover what they would do on a perfect, beautiful Sunday afternoon. She wore her dark hair loose because she'd had it in long braids the day before in their cooking class. Wanting to look her best, she wore a bohemian skirt and blouse with adorable walking boots that she knew were awfully cute and comfortable for their walk. She spied Owen sitting on the designated bench and lit up, waving, as she approached him.

"*Bonjour*, Owen!" She smiled at him deliriously, realizing he looked even cuter today.

"*Bonjour*, Bijoux! Thanks for coming. Let's sit down here for a minute, I want to talk to you."

Happy to oblige, she caught her breath and sat next to him. She bit her bottom lip as he bowed his head and took her hand like it was the most natural move in the world. His boyish head of windblown hair fell into his face, and he shook it away and smiled. "I was so happy to meet you yesterday. I'm not kidding when I say that I had a great time getting to know you in class. But there's something I didn't tell you because I didn't know how you'd react. I thought, if we got to know each other better first, it might be easier for you to believe me."

Bijoux felt her heart drop slightly and removed her hand. "Well what is it?"

"I'm not a student at the school. I only arranged to be in that class yesterday to meet you."

"What?" she said, shocked, and her face reddened.

Owen put his hand on his heart. "Okay, so I've got this long story, and I'm doing this badly. If you'll give me like five minutes of your time, I swear I'll tell you everything and, hopefully, you'll understand."

Owen looked at her and softened his eyes. "But first, I want to say I'm sorry. I hope you'll accept my apology for not being forthright."

She shrugged, uncertain if she should just leave, but Owen didn't seem to be threatening. Far from it. And they were in a very public place. "I don't understand."

"Right, so here goes: I actually work with Homeland Security. I was asked to approach you to see if you'd help us with a delicate problem."

Bijoux had a heavy feeling in her stomach as she moved farther away from him down the bench.

He held up a hand. "You're safe with me. Really. I'm not a bad guy or anything. The opposite, but the situation is...a little tricky." He relaxed into the bench and scratched his head in thought. She couldn't help herself; it almost made her swoon.

"Before I lay it out," he continued, "I'd like to know if you're the type of girl who can keep a secret. You know, like not tell *anyone*? It's really important. No matter what I tell you, it absolutely must stay a secret. Can we trust you? Can I tell you about my problem? Will you protect me, if I open up to you, Bijoux?"

My God. She nearly melted every time he said her name. At this moment, she realized she was intensely curious about three things: One, what he wanted; two, how long she could keep their conversation going; and three, if he would ever kiss her.

She swallowed like it was a difficult decision and said, "*Oui.* Yes. I will protect you, Owen, but what is this about?"

"I'll give you a hint in two words. If you're uncomfortable, then you can walk away and forget I ever existed. But if you will stay and hear me out, please know that I'd be grateful." He looked deeply into her eyes and said, "Hyde Sutton."

She felt her breath catch as she pulled back in surprise, but she did not leave. She licked her lips and leaned closer. "What about him?"

"We think he's up to some bad stuff, Bijoux. Criminal, disgusting, illegal activities that we're currently investigating. You and I met yesterday because my agency tracked you down. We know that you live with the Suttons as the daughter's au pair, and we're wondering if you would be willing to help us obtain some information about him. Information that will possibly save many innocent people. I'm sorry again that I tricked you. Do you forgive me?"

She barely knew what to think about this new information on Mr. Sutton. But Owen was so physically close, and he smelled like heaven. She heard herself utter, "*Oui.*"

"Thank you," he said, taking her hand again and rewarding her with a charming smile. "My partner's name is Michael, and he's sitting on that bench, right over there."

What? She forced her head to swivel and saw another man, who smiled and gave a little wave.

"If you'd be willing, we were wondering if the three of us could take a walk or go to a café, somewhere. Anywhere you'd feel safe so we can lay out the problem we're having with your boss and how you might be able to help us."

She pulled her eyes away from Owen's and looked again at the other man dressed nicely in dark trousers and a long-sleeved shirt. He took off his sunglasses and leaned forward, staring at them. *What's happening here? What should I do?*

"Bijoux," Owen said as he stood and extended a hand to pull her up. "Let's walk for a few minutes, maybe over toward Mitzi's across the park? Let me introduce you to Michael, and he can secure us a table on their patio for a pleasant lunch. On the Bureau, of course. What do you say? Will you have lunch with me? Talk to us?"

"*Oui*," was, once again, all she could manage as he continued to hold her hand and guide her over to meet his partner.

WHAT COULD HAVE BEEN a stress-induced lunch was made palatable because of the soft attention and courage Owen inspired in her. Michael also proved to be a gentleman as they laid out the situation and their suspicions that Hyde Sutton was involved in a human trafficking ring. The thought of her twisted employer involved in something so evil frightened her. But it also didn't wholly surprise her.

Owen and Michael claimed to need more information to confirm their suspicions before the various agencies stepped in and made their move to shut it down. They told her Hyde Sutton was involved, either directly or indirectly, but they wanted to get it right before they moved in. They needed to be careful so they could save as many of the human captives as possible.

After frankly admitting to her that what they were doing and what they were asking her to do was illegal, they explained that they worked for a small part of the organization that everyone knew, but no one spoke about. Similar to spies, Michael and Owen took turns explaining that they did what their country needed them to do without the court orders, without waiting for the slow process of the law, and without the inevitable lawyering that would take place. When called, their department just did the right thing, but it was secret because some illegal tactics were involved.

Owen took a small sip of coffee and said, "We understand that you only have eight months left on your visa here before you need to return to France. Yesterday, you told me about your dream to become a real chef, a trained chef from the CIA, in California, in St. Helena. Is that right? What if I told you that we could arrange for that to happen?"

Bijoux's heartbeat quickened, startled that they knew so much about her and, also, by Owen's intense, soothing proximity. The words of her unspoken dreams, effortlessly pouring out of his seductive mouth felt surreal, but somehow magically blessed.

Owen continued, "Now I'm not saying that it would be immediate, and maybe you would need to return to France for a month or two, but what if we offer you legal assistance with your student visa application and pay for your board and tuition, whether for an associate's or a bachelor's degree out there in the beautiful San Francisco Bay Area. As a reward for your help. What would you say then, Bijoux? This is very important work, but we realize it will come with some anxiety. We'd like to compensate you for it, and we'll be happy to do that in exchange for doing what we ask. The biggest reward, of course, would be that you could close your eyes at night with the knowledge that you did the *right thing* and helped save a bunch of innocent women... maybe even children. Bijoux, will you help us?"

"*Oui*," she said as tears of mixed emotions slowly slid down her face. "I want to help you and to help the women, but how do I know for sure that what you're telling me, this terrible story is the truth? What if this is *business* spying and you're tricking me? What if I get caught doing these illegal activities? I want to help you, but how can I be sure?"

Owen looked over to Michael, who gave him a small nod.

Owen turned to her and reached for her hand under the table. "That's an excellent question, and I think it speaks highly of your character that you wouldn't help us expose Hyde just for the money. But Mr. Sutton is doing business with some extremely dangerous people, and we think the less you know the better. That said, I could show you videotape evidence of a boatload of women we believe are victims in this trafficking ring. If you'd like, we can leave here and go somewhere private where you can view it. The important part to remember is that the women are being taken off a boat onto a pier that belongs to Mr. Hyde Sutton. He owns it and controls it. You can make your own determinations about what you're seeing.

"In America, there are laws. If you get into a car with someone, and they commit a crime—say a drive-by shooting—even if you didn't know about it and weren't the shooter, you would still be considered guilty. It is no different with this case, but we need to get more evidence and understand Hyde's involvement, so he doesn't get away with it. Any audio and videotapes, his e-mails, and other items we recover may or may not be used against him down the road, but the information will surely help us stop the operation and make the people responsible pay for their crimes. Mr. Sutton included."

Owen smiled tenderly. "You're not alone, Bijoux. If anything happens, you can call me or Michael, anytime, day or night, and we'll pick you up and protect you. Legally and physically. You have my word."

Mesmerized and intrigued, but terribly nervous, she dabbed at her eyes. *Did he say he'd pick me up in the middle of the night?*

"Mr. Sutton leaves for Russia tomorrow. Pravdina has appointments for shopping and Simone will be in school. Will you help me with the technology, or do I do this by myself?"

"Does he have security cameras in the apartment?"

"No, not that I know of."

Owen nodded. "It's not a problem. We can jam the feeds and create interference to be on the safe side. So yes, I can come to you at the apartment and plant the devices. You won't have to do anything other than let me in. I'll need about an hour to get everything planted. Do you happen to know which network Hyde uses for his phone and Internet?"

Still trembly, she relaxed a bit, knowing they wouldn't require her to really do anything. "Yes. They have Verizon, whole house. Televisions, phones, computers; they gave me a phone to use that has this service."

"Okay. Do you know how long Hyde will be gone?"

"They say one week. He leaves tomorrow."

"Pravdina isn't going to Russia with him? You'd think with her language background she could be helpful to him."

"Mrs. Sutton does not like to travel. I think she likes her time alone when Mr. Sutton is away. It is restful for her."

"All right." Owen looked at Michael. "Why don't you go back to the office and grab your iPad so we can show Bijoux the video of the hostages. When he gets back, you can watch it, and I'm confident that what you'll see will make you want to help these unfortunate women. We'll give you a burner phone to contact us, and tomorrow, once you give me the all clear, I'll come over to set up the apartment. Do you agree?"

"I'm very frightened; this is happening so fast."

"I know it must be overwhelming, but I can't tell you how important this mission is for us. I have your back here, I promise you. We all do. But remember, we're going out on a limb here, as well, hoping we can trust you."

She nodded in understanding. "But how long will the surveillance take? Will he look for bugs if he gets suspicious? What then?"

"One step at a time. We have a plan, Bijoux, but the first step starts with you."

"You can trust me, Owen." She smiled.

He rewarded her with a charming smile, dimples showing, and reached over and kissed her hand. "And you can trust me, too. Thank you for your help."

Chapter 18

MACCHI & MACCHI had a productive week while Hyde was out of town. They rented one of the smaller apartments in Sutton Tower, three floors below the penthouse, for an enormous amount of money. The real estate agents had been agreeable once they realized that there was very little downside to a six-month, all-cash lease. The approval of their application was pushed through under an alias, and the huge upfront security deposit, along with a morality clause, gave the agents peace of mind that it was a short-term win-win.

The main Macchi crew—Michael, Alex, and obviously Charlotte—could not be seen anywhere in the vicinity of Sutton Tower, so they moved Karla Fernandez and another employee Danny Roe in. Posing as a married couple, they moved into the space to keep tabs on the penthouse action and to disseminate the information.

Minimal furnishings were brought in and Karla and Danny took turns with the tedious work, only leaving the apartment for food or supplies. Their security setup was tight, and no one else in the building would ever know what they were doing. The highly illegal interceptor with the long-range antenna was working perfectly, giving them a base station three floors below Hyde's apartment. While Hyde was in the apartment, they could sync up to his phone, listen in to his calls, and receive his text messages.

Another electronic option was discussed and rejected. Owen had explained the technology process for cloning Hyde's phone, but that would require Bijoux to be alone with the phone for ten minutes. She told them she didn't think that opportunity would arise, as he always had it with him or next to his bedside—and she had absolutely no desire or reason to enter that area of the home.

That setback aside, Bijoux had given Owen advice about the areas of the home where Hyde would normally conduct his business, and Owen successfully planted bugs in his office, living room, and dining room, which gave them live audio and visual into those areas. He also successfully downloaded the contents of Hyde's home computer, which was shipped off to Bacon to gather any pertinent e-mails or information. He installed a backdoor into the computer that would give Bacon real-time access to watch Hyde's activities while he was using that desktop. All in all, the Macchi & Macchi crew was doing fine surveillance work in both his home and at the Bay Ridge complex.

It had been Michael Macchi's job to bring in the cops, which was tricky. Macchi & Macchi was working in an illegal capacity, spying on Hyde Sutton and acquiring reams of information from an illegal hacker and surveillance equipment. This made the full disclosure of the operation impossible. But over the years, the firm had developed strong relationships with many individuals and agencies in law enforcement. If what they believed was happening was real, then Hyde Sutton was involved in a human trafficking ring that might also involve transnational gang activity. Michael and Alex agreed that they needed to tap their contact in Homeland Security, Clarence Beutz.

A security investigator who they'd worked with in the past, Clarence was in an authority position to have some flexibility to overlook the questionable legalities of his sources and focus on the valuable security information that came to them.

The brothers asked Clarence to meet with them on their turf in the Macchi & Macchi offices, where they could detect or jam any electronic equipment Clarence could be carrying that might expose—or God forbid—trap them, if some Machiavellian agent saw another opportunity. Fortunately, they believed Clarence was one of the good guys, and he'd never betrayed their trust in the past. They hoped that goodwill would continue, but they had to prepare for the worst.

Escorted into the safe and comfortable environs of Alex's office—most definitely not the war room—Clarence greeted the brothers warmly.

"By the look on your faces," Clarence said, clearly enjoying their discomfort, "I can see you might be in a quandary? What? Does this mean that, in the course of your illegal activities, you've once again stumbled over something you shouldn't have? Do you need police interference or legal advice today, gentleman?"

Looking across the small conference table to their associate from Homeland Security, Alex thought Clarence looked an awful lot like both a cop and lawyer. Tall, fit, and athletic, the man also had the look of a bookworm lawyer with his suit and spectacles.

Alex cleared his throat and began, "We wouldn't turn away the free legal advice, Clarence, but this would be more of an intel kind of a meeting. We do have some information that we stumbled across, but before we share it with you, I hope, as usual, that we can count on your discretion and protection of us as the source. Those parameters are what allow us to come to you openly without fear of reprisal. But we're still going out on a limb. The fact is, we've come across a tragic situation and discovered a human trafficking ring in Bay Ridge. We'd like your help to shut it down."

Clarence sat up straighter. "I'm listening. Why don't you start from the beginning; maybe tell me who your client is?"

Michael jumped in, "I can tell you the name of the man involved—Hyde Sutton. We think he's involved with the Russian mafia, giving them access to a port in the harbor so they can smuggle women into the country."

Clarence's eyes opened wide. "Whoa, whoa, whoa. Hyde Sutton?" His head swiveled between them. "You've got to be kidding me."

Alex crossed his legs and sat back, his mouth in a tight line. "I'm not. I'll briefly take you through the chain of events that led up to this discovery, and we also have a videotape that speaks for itself." He proceeded to give Clarence the intel about the Sutton Tower situation and Hyde's general anger toward the Macchis.

Alex worked his jaw muscles reliving the details and Michael cleared his voice and took over. "We thought we needed to be prepared, so we decided to take a deeper look into Mr. Hyde's life, and by chance, found he has a property,

Bay Ridge Properties, owned by a holding company, *his* holding company, Mercer Investment Group. This particular warehouse complex happens to be located near our mother's home in Bay Ridge. You may remember that our brother, Tony, is a police detective in the 10th Precinct?"

Clarence nodded, tapping his fingers on the table, trying to keep up. Michael continued, telling Clarence about the attack their brother suffered while checking out the property in Bay Ridge owned by Hyde.

Alex took over: "The assault—which we felt wasn't coincidental—influenced us to make the decision that there might be something bigger to investigate over at Bay Ridge Properties. So we set up a bird's nest in a building across the street from the complex. One night, during a fireworks harbor event, a boat pulled up to the pier at the back of the property. This was the first boat we'd seen using the pier at the back of the complex, and our guy in the nest had the presence of mind to record it."

Michael spun a small laptop toward Clarence. "What you'll see on the video is a group of women being unloaded from the boat and roughly transferred into the back of a couple paneled vans. The boat disappears, the vans leave the complex, and it's lights out. Unfortunately, we weren't prepared to follow the vehicles, but we did manage to capture their license numbers and track them as for sale at a used-car lot in Brooklyn. The next day, those vans were back in the lot, still for sale, so we believe they were specifically used just for this transport."

Alex crossed his arms. "In addition, prior to the smuggling event, we discovered that Hyde's Bay Ridge complex is being used as some kind of distribution warehouse with some regular vehicle activity whose registration belongs to a company named Med Source. We discovered that Med Source is a subsidiary of a shell company named ZATO with ties to Mr. Viktor Timofeyev, otherwise known as 'The Arm,' who you probably know is a Russian mafia boss."

They paused to let Clarence absorb what he heard and to close his mouth, which had dropped open.

Clarence finally said, "You don't fuck around when you find a problem do you, boys. The Timofeyevs? Hyde Sutton? Human trafficking? What the hell?" He threw his head back in disbelief. "If what you're telling me is true, then we've got ourselves one big pile of shit to wade through." Clarence scratched at something behind his ear. "This is just unbelievable. God, every time you call me, I don't know if I'm excited to hear from you or horrified."

Alex said in a low, serious voice, "Show him the video, Michael."

After viewing it, Clarence sat back. He closed his eyes and gestured, beginning to formulate a thought and then stopped. "Look," he said finally, "I'm not sure what I saw there, if I'm honest, but my gut tells me that you're right. Something bad's happening there. Damn it, did you get the name of the boat?"

"No," said Alex. "The light was wrong, but we have a general idea about the make and model of the craft, so that's something. We haven't checked into it yet; maybe the Port Authority could help."

"What about the vans? You said they were just sitting in the lot the next day, for sale? Which lot?" He patted his pockets and found his phone, pulled up an app, and began typing.

"Metropolitan Used Cars, in Brooklyn, on Oak. We haven't done anything with that yet either," said Michael.

"We didn't want to alert anyone or spook them. The way we figure, the Russians have some kind of arrangement with the lot or the owner, or they have an inside source willing to loan out some vans for a night of illegal transport. Maybe the guy is being extorted and looks the other way; who knows? But the vans can't be tied to ZATO or Timofeyev in a traditional manner."

Clarence threw up his hands. "Shit, I'm going to have to bring Immigrations and Customs Enforcement into this. ICE has a task force dedicated to human trafficking, and if that's what we think is happening, then they need in on it too."

"What about Hyde?" Alex leaned forward.

Clarence paused, the anger in Alex's voice apparent. "Alex, I don't know Mr. Sutton personally, but I've heard rumors that he's not a great guy to work for. Cutthroat businessman. It's Manhattan. Some people respect that, even admire it, but if he's out there abusing women, then he's just another piece of shit, and I'd like to nail him. The thing is, if this blows up and if he's brought into it, then it's going to get legally ugly. Really ugly, and that's what the justice department is for. I can't predict what'll happen to him. I believe you when you say it's his property, but Hyde may not have knowledge or direct involvement, so I just don't know."

"It's his complex!" Alex said vehemently, pounding his index finger on the table. "He pays the taxes. His company, Mercer Investment Group, owns it. He receives no recorded income from the use of it by Med Source, Timofeyev, or anyone else, but the Russians have the keys. The Russian mafia uses the place, for God knows what else, but now we believe they're smuggling in sex slaves."

Alex pointed the finger in Clarence's face. "Hyde gave them the keys to a port of entry in *New York Harbor* and walked away. No restrictions, just a nice, quiet little vetted pier to load and unload in the dead of night. Hyde Sutton owns it, and that makes him both complicit and guilty."

Clarence put up a hand. "I agree with you, Alex. I do. I'm just warning you that the lawyers and the Justice Department have their own world—the courts—which isn't my area. I want to catch the bad guys, and I want to make it stick, so I'm going to focus on my end. I'll need to bring in some more people, and we need a plan. I gotta talk to my boss so we do this thing right. One step at a time. Carefully—so no one, and that includes Hyde if he's in on this, walks away."

"And the women," said Michael. "Our first priority is to find them and help them. We believe that this was not a one-off; there will be another shipment, or movement, or something. Next time we want to be in place to follow them."

Clarence shook his head. "Whoa, slow it down. If what we have here is the Russian mafia, then, no offense, but you do not have the authority to burst in like the cavalry, guns drawn, and rescue them. That would be our job."

"Exactly." Michael nodded. "And we're counting on you to do it and to protect us when you explain how we found out. We don't want any subpoenas, press, or notoriety on this. Our business is security and deep, dark background. We are not the glory guys; you can take the credit because we need to have a long leash with no eyes to do our job well. Do we have your word that you'll do what you can to protect us?"

Clarence looked between them and nodded. "You do. Because if I can predict what's going to happen next, we're going to need to work together at your surveillance hutch and coordinate the takedown. We'll want to round up all the bad guys at the same time; it's the only way the operation doesn't just move across town. We need to get as many of the players as we can in one fell swoop, so we're going to proceed carefully."

Alex turned his head, but not before a look of disgust passed over it.

Clarence said, "Alex, we are going to help. You have my word. We appreciate what you do here, and I've come to respect both of you guys. So let's get this moving and see what we can do together."

Alex didn't respond as Clarence and Michael got up. He stayed silent as his brother escorted Clarence out of the offices.

"Why didn't you tell him what he did to Charlotte," Michael asked, once he was back.

"Because it's bad enough that Clarence already believes we have a personal vendetta against Hyde over the contractors' thing and Tony. If something should happen to Mr. Hyde, I don't want Clarence to view us as suspects. I suppose that might be inevitable, but why give them anything more than we have to. Besides, it's Charlotte's decision who she chooses to tell."

Michael nodded. "I think we can trust them. The Justice Department will sort it out after we close down the port. Hyde—Mercer, owns it. Roman Timofeyev is a partner in Mercer. They'll link it back to him. Hyde will be pulled apart by the legal system over this one. The FBI, the New

York Port Authority, none of those guys are pushovers, you know that."

Alex got up and went to a window. "But Hyde's slippery, Michael, and he has huge amounts of money to throw at the problem to make it go away. He'll push back on all the agencies and blame everything on the Russians. I can just see it. It's not going to hurt him. Not like I want it to. *We* need to do that. We'll help the cops do their job, and I feel good that they'll be on this—I do. That's the most important part, shutting this down.

"But. Hyde—he's ours. It's up to us to make sure he doesn't slip off the hook. And what we need is an insurance policy."

Alex smiled as he moved over to the sofa and sat back. He rested one arm over the back as he picked up his tie and smoothed it. "The Justice Department will be required to jump through all the legal hoops, but we know someone who would be happy to work around that and take care of Hyde personally. Viktor Timofeyev. When the shit hits the fan and his operation comes apart, we need to make sure 'The Arm' believes it was Hyde Sutton who brought him down."

Alex raised an eyebrow and glowed. "This shit storm is going to make Viktor Timofeyev a very angry man, so let's just point him and his anger in the right direction. We'll *inspire* 'The Arm' to take care of Mr. Hyde—for all of us."

Alex gave Michael a gleeful smile. It was coming together nicely.

Chapter 19

THREE FLOORS BELOW Hyde Sutton's penthouse apartment, Karla Fernandez nursed a beer while watching Hyde Sutton strut to and fro in his home office, in front of a 10' x 10' garishly beveled, gold plated mirror. The man himself, just back from his trip to St. Petersburg, Russia, conducted a series of ridiculous poses, unaware that Karla and the Macchi & Macchi team had a front-row seat for the show.

Hyde admired his image wearing a full-length, vintage, red-velvet smoking jacket, while conducting business on the phone with his lawyer, Thaddeus Brothers.

"It was a good trip, real good. I don't usually fly with the public airlines, but first class wasn't all bad. They've got some nice-looking broads. Everything looks like it's supposed to at this stage. Our architect met with their guys on the ground. The Russians—they don't have anything on us, I can tell you that. Worlds apart in their operations over there. Don't know their shit from Shinola, but they'll get the job done."

Karla watched Hyde switch to different colored slippers as he continued his lecture. "Roman says he's got it locked down. I guess his father is pulling some strings. Now there's a guy you don't want to meet in a back alley. Real rough-looking guy. Big. Huge. I'm talking fat. Met him at Roman's before we left for Russia. Roman's got a pipsqueak place in Brooklyn. Nice enough if you're middle class, but I couldn't live over there. His father, Viktor, he and I got along good though. By the end of it, I had him eating out of the palm of my hand. Guy was a street punk, I'm thinking. Russian thug and absolutely no class. You should have seen what he was wearing. Huge, *huge* gold chains. Jesus what a throwback. But hey, what do I care what he looks like as long as his people get the job done. That's how it works over there. Thug to thug. Let them battle it out, just as long as they don't think they can screw me over. Nobody can. That's for sure. Right, Thad?"

Karla put back the rest of her beer, recognizing a monologue when she heard one. Hyde's lawyer was probably doing the same.

"Speaking of thugs...what's the latest with the Macchi lawsuits? I hope you're crushing those assholes at Baach. Take the time you need, but hear me, we don't negotiate. We're not giving them a penny. Not a goddamned penny to those asshole subcontractors. Let 'em rot. The Macchis too. Let them throw their money to the lawyers. It'll serve them right for getting involved in this."

Hyde sat on the corner of his desk and struck a different pose in the mirror as he continued, "In the meantime, I've got to focus on the deal with the Russians. Roman and I met with his partners on the ground in St. Petersburg, and one guy, oligarch type, there's another one. Had on this polyester, *polyester*, for God sake. I am not shitting you. This shirt? All shiny and he had way too many extra buttons open, like what, we all wanted to see his jungle of chest hair? What the fuck is wrong with these people? But hey, not everyone can have class. Just as long as this deal makes us money, that's all I care about. I'll deal with the goddamned devil if it makes me money, and from the looks of them, I might not be too far off. But if the numbers are right, we're going to be sitting pretty with this one. It's going to be huge for us. Huge. Roman said we should get over to Prague in September, so that one's coming along too."

Three floors below, Karla rubbed her temples as the night wore on. Duly recording the entire conversation and watching and listening in live time, if at points it could be considered grotesquely entertaining, it got truly sickening later in the evening as Hyde and Pravdina had what could only be described as a "fashion orgy."

Pravdina had been ordered into the office along with a rack of evening gowns and accessories so they could decide together which outfit she should wear to the upcoming Sloan Kettering Ball. Hyde had her, mostly, naked in heels as she slipped into one dress after another. He would then choose from the accessory options and critique her in a demeaning manner.

"This one makes your ass look huge," he said, giving it an audible smack. "Jesus, Prav, look at that. Do you see that?" He grabbed a handful of her ass cheek hard and shook it. "You've got a solid-gold ass, and the drape of this one makes it look like your smuggling something under there! I don't want your ass to get any bigger, do you hear me? I know big asses are trending, but I don't like it. You tell that bitch of a stylist that we don't want to see anything that makes your ass look big. You tell him that, or I will. As a matter of fact, I'll text that bitch now. This designer doesn't know what he's doing. That cut, it makes the gown *actually enhance* your ass. You see that? It makes it look huge. What a ridiculous trend. Thank God you have me around to help you avoid these mistakes, Prav. You're one lucky girl, you know that?

"Look at us! Together, we're like the sexiest couple in the world. I grant you, that it's mostly your looks that bring us over the top, but when people see me, they think power. Bam! Power. Rich. Important. Then they look at you and think: *He can afford that because he's the best. He's a man who has it all.* I swear to God if we don't make this season's best-dressed list, I'm going to kill that editor at *Vanity Fair*. I swear to God, that little asshole. He knows I have more class in my little finger than he has in his entire body, and it makes him jealous. It's all about petty jealousies when you get to the top. So we have to impress everyone. We can never, *you* can never, *never*, let your guard down. You always need to look your best. It's our hallmark. My trademark. Everyone looks at us when we walk into the room, and when they do, I want their goddamned eyes to pop open and their mouths to hit the floor when they see us. So don't disappoint me, Prav. And that goes for Simone too. You keep on top of her!"

And on it went. For hours. Karla felt incredibly creepy watching the woman walk around naked and knew that she would be flagging that portion of the video from the rest of the staff so she could protect Pravdina from the personal invasion she didn't know she was experiencing. It was bad enough that her husband treated her like a live mannequin and barely let an opinion escape her lips unchecked, but the way he spoke to her was shocking. When they'd planted the recording equipment, they purposefully left the bedrooms alone to avoid this type of inappropriate surveillance. What they didn't know at the time was that Hyde used his office—typically in front of the large mirror—to conduct his extracurricular activities.

By the end of the fashion show, Karla had turned off the visual monitors. Although still recording, she didn't want to watch the further sexual humiliation that Hyde Sutton was making his wife endure.

It was a long evening for all of them, and Karla felt great sympathy for Pravdina Sutton. The woman was paying an enormous price for every luxurious advantage she had. Not in a million years would Karla ever believe that the life she lived was happy and fulfilling. She would never understand why someone would marry a man like Hyde Sutton and put up with his behavior. She'd make sure her report highlighted the fact that Pravdina was probably not a happy wife.

Chapter 20

THE NEXT DAY Alex sat with Michael in the war room, looking over Karla's latest report. "They're going to the Sloan Kettering Ball; it's like two weeks from now. Maybe we could do something there," Michael mused.

The conversation was interrupted by Danny Roe, who had the day shift on the Sutton Tower surveillance. Alex put the call on speaker. "Guys," said Danny, "you can watch the video yourself, but I wanted to let you know what I heard them discussing this morning as soon as possible."

"What have you got?" asked Michael.

"Simone, Hyde, and Pravdina were having a family breakfast in the dining room; Bijoux was serving. All kinds of weird shit was going down, no kidding, including Hyde making a lewd gesture with his tongue to Bijoux while no one was looking. Man, really sick. Anyway, Hyde makes his wife and daughter stand, and he does a critique on their outfits, which was another awkward moment, but then he starts complimenting his daughter on her great figure. The girl is eleven, right? Talking about how proud he is of her that she's so slim and eats like a bird, that boys like that. The anorexic pep talk went on for a while and the mom, she's trying to talk, but Hyde just keeps at it and babbles over her. But then, Hyde starts talking to Simone about Petunia."

Alex darkened; his hackles rose as he leaned in. "What did he say, Danny?"

"He told Simone that he felt sorry for her. Alex, I don't want to be repeating this shit, so I apologize, but I thought you'd want to know. He was going on about her looks, her dancing ability, her tragic father...you can imagine. He was painting a terrible picture about her and your family. He said that he knew—that it was fact and known all over town—that you were having an affair, and the family was in big trouble. 'Like a house of cards,' he said. Financial, everything. He said it was only a matter of time before it all came down on you. He told Simone to feel sorry for Petunia, and then sort of suggested that she put out the word to the other girls at the academy that they should keep an eye out on her too. Like watch for the inevitable—and I'm quoting here: 'suicidal breakdown, because it's coming.'"

Alex rubbed his mouth with his fist, trying to stay calm, his skin prickling with the first rushes of adrenaline.

"I'm really sorry, Alex, but I thought you'd want to know," said Danny.

"Is he still in the apartment?" Michael asked.

"No, he left after breakfast, right after giving his family instructions to go out and make the Sutton name proud."

"Okay, Danny. I'm glad you called. Let us know if you hear anything else," said Michael. Alex gritted his teeth and glared at Michael, who shot him a look to stay calm and counseled him quietly: "Come on, Alex, we knew the man was scum. We knew that. Everything already supported it, so even though it's hard to hear, we really shouldn't be surprised."

Alex nodded. "No. You're right. We shouldn't be, but I guess I fucking am anyway. 'Suicidal breakdown?' I want to fucking kill him."

"Shut that shit down, Alex," Michael said firmly.

Alex ran his hands through his hair and tried to keep focused. "Charlotte and I gotta prepare Petunia tonight. In the meantime, find out if Roman Timofeyev will also be attending the Sloan Kettering Ball. If he is, then we need to be there as well."

"You and Charlotte?" Michael got up and wrote some details on the whiteboard.

Alex squinted, considering. "No. You know what? I think we need to send Owen and a sloppy, big-mouthed date. We need to bring in a ringer, and I have the perfect candidate in mind. But before the ball, we need to get Owen and Hyde in the same room. They need to meet each other before they reunite at the Sloan Kettering thing."

Michael rubbed his hands. "I think I know where you're going with this. We know Hyde is in town, so all we have to do is convince him to take a meeting with Owen. It doesn't have to be for long; Owen just needs the face time with him. How are we going to get Hyde to take a meeting? Who do we say is calling? We don't have much time before the ball."

Alex flexed his hands. "We play to his ego. Get Owen in here, and let's set this up today."

Chapter 21

THEY DISCOVERED THAT Roman Timofeyev would be attending the ball as a singleton, sharing a table with Hyde and Pravdina Sutton. With that confirmed, it was full steam ahead and time to introduce Owen Kai to Hyde.

Strategizing in the war room with Michael and Owen, Alex thought they had a good plan. Owen was a capable guy, and Alex was glad they had him on the team. He slid a piece of paper with Hyde's cell number on it over to his happy-go-lucky lothario. "You shouldn't have any problems. Experience tells me that dropping, 'Homeland Security' has a tendency to open doors."

A side of Owen's mouth turned up. "Uh huh. So now I'm once again illegally impersonating a federal officer. How many laws are we breaking on this one?"

Alex stared down his employee ready to object, but Owen smiled and shrugged. "Just kidding, man. I'm not losing any sleep over this one."

Owen tossed his hair back and placed the call. "Mr. Sutton?" Owen said in a pleasant manner.

"Who is this?" Hyde's voice came over the speaker and into the war room. He sounded confused.

"Mr. Sutton, my name is Inspector Daniel Parks, I'm an agent with Homeland Security. I was wondering if I could have a few moments of your time?"

"What do you want? Who gave you this number?" Hyde sounded irritated.

Owen cleared his throat. "I'm sure you understand that finding your cell number was not difficult, but I promise I won't be sharing it with anyone outside of the agency. We were wondering if you'd be willing to meet us this afternoon at your office. We have something important to discuss. We won't need more than ten minutes of your time."

"How do I know you're not some nut job?"

Alex rolled his eyes as Owen continued in a serious voice. "I think I'll be able to reassure you this afternoon. Are you interested in protecting your homeland, Mr. Sutton? Because I have it directly from our mayor that you're a man of integrity who we could count on for help. I'll explain everything this afternoon. Would you be available at four?"

"The mayor? Sure. Four o'clock. My office. I suppose you know where to find me."

"We do. I look forward to meeting with you then, sir."

Owen glanced up with a satisfied look as he disconnected the call. "How did I do?" Alex stood to leave, furious after hearing Hyde's smarmy voice. "Alex?" Owen said.

"You did fine," Alex had to get some air. He walked out, slamming the door behind him.

Chapter 22

Hyde sat in his Sutton Tower office and scrolled through his Twitter feed, following a disturbing story about a woman running for New York City mayor. He'd seen the ugly broad at parties and couldn't believe she had so many supporters. He tossed off a tweet calling her "Boozin' Susan" and "a fat, incompetent hack." No way she was going to replace his guy. Not if he had anything to say about it. He smiled, knowing his nickname for her would trend.

Interrupted by his secretary at precisely 4:00 p.m., he gave her the green light to let the Homeland Security guys into his office. He couldn't imagine what the meeting would be about.

Hyde stood behind his desk as two well-suited men with nearly matching red ties were escorted into his imposing, gleaming inner sanctum and marched confidently up to him. The better-looking one extended his hand over the desk, saying, "Mr. Sutton. Daniel Parks. It's an honor to meet you, sir. Thank you for making the time to see us. This is my partner in Homeland Security, Inspector Hill."

Hyde shook the hands and said, "All right, so what's on your mind? Did someone in my organization do something, 'cause I can tell you, we're extremely careful that we don't hire the wrong kind of people around here. No illegals. No questionable characters. We're extremely careful on that front."

Hyde took a seat at his desk as Daniel Parks and his partner got comfortable in their chairs. Daniel/Owen began, "No sir, nothing like that. I'm sure you have an exceptional vetting process here. In fact, I understand that you have an exemplary organization run by a leader with great love for his country. No, the reason we're here, Mr. Sutton," he continued, "is that we wanted to make you aware of a Homeland program that encourages partnership between our people and the heads of all the largest businesses in the country. In New York City, it's our job to meet with the top people, the movers and the shakers with access to people we normally wouldn't. We need them to keep an open ear and help us keep our city safe."

Hyde folded his hands on his desk. He stuck out his bottom lip as he listened with interest to the unusual offer.

"A man in your position, naturally, does a huge amount of business with unions and contractors—all sorts of individuals who, in turn, have their own networks. My partner and I are only approaching the *biggest* players in the city, directly, to see if we can count on their support. In fact, as a show of goodwill, we're launching a new proactive means of enhancing these communications by offering rewards for leads. We're offering up to $1 million for the right leads, but we need to keep a tight lid on that. We're not approaching *everyone*, Mr. Sutton. God knows there are some people out there who would try to take advantage of the reward system or give us false leads to discredit a competitor. No, we're vetting our sources carefully. Your name was at the top of the list of people we know we can trust. We're only approaching men with the highest integrity, with the very best reputations for making this city the greatest in the nation."

Hyde Sutton sat back, relaxed and gratified to hear his reputation was firmly established and that his close connection to the mayor was once again paying off. "I'm glad to hear that you're being progressive out there, but hasn't there been a rewards program in place since 9/11?"

Daniel nodded. "Yes sir. The Rewards for Justice Program has been around for a while, and we've been fairly successful in arresting terrorists before they've committed acts. In fact, we've probably awarded close to $200 million for those leads with the biggest bounties on the heads of the people deemed 'most wanted' by the State Department. That program is still in place, but what we're trying to achieve locally, on U.S. soil, is a continued awareness that the program exists, that we would be grateful for any assistance, and the rewards will be paid. Most of the money awarded through RFJ has been for information leading to *convictions*, but with this new program, we're not only keeping that in place, but also adding rewards for solid leads, even if they are, ultimately, not convicted in a court of law."

Hyde rocked and considered: *The guy's hair is a little long for a Fed, but who knows how the government really works? Talk about a chaos-ripe organization filled with opportunities.*

The Parks guy pressed on: "Not everyone has built empires, Mr. Sutton. Not everyone has access to such a broad spectrum of people, and Joe Average will probably never be in a position to help keep America safe, but you will. God willing, you will never come up against a real terrorist, but as a part of our job, we wanted to remind you that we are out there; we are interested; and we will pay. Consider this visit no more than a pop-up ad, reminding you that we appreciate all the help we can get."

"All right, I'll keep my eyes open."

"We knew we could count on you, sir." Daniel stood and handed him a card. "Here's the number of the hotline at Homeland. They'll connect you to me if you'd ever like to speak. In the meantime," Daniel leaned over the desk to shake Hyde's hand, "we've taken up enough of your valuable time. When I said we would only need ten minutes, sir, I meant it. We wouldn't want to inconvenience you further."

Hyde stood, while shaking Daniel's hand; he then watched the two men bow their heads and walk out of the room. He wasn't sure what to make of it, but all in a day. He'd seen his share of just about everything now and wasn't surprised by much. It was good to know they were still working their jobs. He wondered who else in the city was getting a visit. *Damn, I should have asked.*

Chapter 23

"SO TONIGHT'S THE NIGHT. You ready?" Alex rubbed his hands together as he and Owen sat in the open great room of his temporary home on Park Avenue.

It was a warm July evening and Owen, dapper and tuxedoed, smiled at Lily who was sitting nearby, surrounded by her dolls.

"No problem, Alex. I got this."

Lily, all of two, smiled shyly at Owen, while Alex considered the plan they'd made for the evening to come.

The Memorial Sloan Kettering Ball was considered one of New York society's most prestigious fundraising events. Raising millions of dollars each year for the world-renowned cancer center, obtaining tickets to the gala on such short notice had proved difficult, even for Charlotte. Attending the event wasn't the problem, it was getting a seat at one of the tables that had long been sold out. However, after she had lunch with the one of the organizers and pledged a very generous donation, two seats were made available for the newly minted Homeland Security Inspector Daniel Parks and his date, flown in specifically for the event, Carey Carrows.

As they watched the sun set on the Manhattan skyline, Alex counseled Owen on his clandestine job for the evening. "Carey's a pro, Owen. I know you've never met her, but there's no need to worry; she'll deliver the lines to Roman. All you need to do is let her work the room to get to him and then discreetly make yourself scarce once she has his undivided attention. It would be perfect if you could be seen speaking with Hyde at the same time. If for some reason that doesn't work, we'll find a Plan B. In the meantime, Carey will keep her eyes peeled on your movements and will plant the appropriate seed with Roman."

Owen nodded. "I get the plan. You've gone over everything with her? Does she know about the operation in its entirety and about the abducted women?"

Alex thought about the nature of the conversation and glanced nervously at Lily who was stacking her dolls on their heads near a window. "She does. Charlotte and her family are very close; they don't keep secrets from one another. What you say to one, you're probably saying to all of them. Now Carey—I suppose you've seen pictures of her?"

Owen brightened, glancing expectantly down the hallway, apparently anxious for her to make her appearance. "She's damn beautiful, Alex."

Alex rolled his shoulders and grimaced slightly, thinking about Carey and her unexpected nature. "She is. But heed this slight warning: she's a bit unpredictable. And, uh, as your boss here, I don't want you to feel, that is, if she were to, make advances, it would be totally up to you about how you want to handle it. Make sure she understands that you're not her personal plaything. She's there to do a job, just like you. Consider yourself warned, Owen. We'll not be entertaining any sexual harassment suits after tonight."

Owen smiled and straightened his bow tie. "I'm not terribly worried about that end, besides, we'll be in public for most of the evening,"

"Yes, well, I'll not disillusion you about what I've seen her accomplish in public. You're both adults, that's all I'm saying."

"Is she seeing anyone right now?" Owen whispered.

Alex shook his head. "On any given day, I have no idea. Here they come."

He and Owen stood as platinum-blonde Carey Carrows entered the room like a lithe, exotic feline. Alex had learned quite a lot about fashion and recognized the features of the pale-blue, fully beaded, sleeveless evening gown. With a V neckline, empire waist, and deeply draped cowl back, the astoundingly delicate dress shimmered an iridescent blue. Pooling with a small back train, she wore pale-blue diamond and aquamarine earrings and an enormous matching ring. From a distance, she looked naked beneath the beads, but the dress was lined with a nude sheath that matched her skin.

Charlotte followed her younger sister into the room and smiled as they watched the irresistible ladies' man, Owen Kai, openly gape at Carey.

"Well, boys," said Carey, doing a slow turn and giving a coquettish smile over her shoulder. "What do you think? Do I look all right for the job?"

Alex cleared his throat. "Owen Kai," he said, extending his arm. "May I present my sister-in-law, Carey Carrows."

Owen had a 10,000-watt smile plastered on his face as he approached and accepted her hand. "Carey. Carey Carrows. It's a pleasure to meet you. You look like a dream," he said as he bent and kissed her hand.

Charlotte glanced at Alex and gave him some wide eyes. Most likely, she was also reacting to the heat emanating from the couple. Alex didn't know whether to smile or throw a blanket over his impressionable two-year old who was watching. The air felt electrically charged as the chemistry around the couple crackled.

"Thank you," said Carey. "You look very handsome yourself. Charlotte tells me you're single. Is that true?"

Charlotte jumped in, "Oh, I hope you don't mind, Owen. I know it's none of my business, but she asked, and I..."

The couple was staring, running their eyes over one another as if they were dessert. "It's perfectly fine, Charlotte," Owen said over his shoulder, not taking his eyes off Carey. "It's true. And may I ask if you're seeing anyone special, Carey?"

Carey took his arm and turned him to leave the room. "You're the only special person in sight, Owen."

As they walked toward the door Alex called out, "Ah, remember, his name isn't Owen tonight, guys. It's Daniel Parks!"

Alex couldn't be sure they heard him as he and Charlotte watched them leave without so much as a backward glance. After the door closed, Charlotte put a hand on her chest and swooned. "Did you see that dress. It was a Naeem Khan—and the most modest one that she brought. I had a heck of time getting her out of the Jason Wu. That was just a sheer gown, totally nude with allover floral appliques. Believe me, from the back, it left *nothing* to the imagination. My God, this gala has such a conservative crowd."

Alex smiled. "There'll be plenty of doctors at the Sloan Kettering Ball should anyone, including Owen, have need of resuscitation."

Charlotte brightened. "They seemed to like each other, didn't they? No one can say they're not a gorgeous couple."

Alex glanced at the front door. "No. No one could say that. But I wonder if Owen may have finally met his match."

CAREY THOUGHT OWEN was one of the best-looking men she'd ever seen and felt herself exhibiting uncharacteristic blushes on the drive to the hotel. He almost made her feel shy, and no one did that. Looking like a combination of Keanu Reeves with the deep-brown eyes of Josh Hartnett, he was not classically beautiful, but definitely had a face filled with mischief. She adored the fact that he seemed willing to play.

Arriving at the Plaza Hotel, the town car pulled to the front to drop them off. Owen hopped out, came around to her door, and extended his hand to help her out. He didn't let go, however, and she glanced down at their entwined hands and gave him a side smile as they entered the lobby together. He seemed to appreciate the look and broke out in a boyish grin.

They walked into the fashionably elegant ballroom; the place glittered with dazzling decorations and people. A band played lively music as they made their way through the crowd and found their seats at a tastefully decorated table for twelve. The two of them wandered around, mingling lightly with the moneyed and celebrity crowd, dutifully getting a lay of the land.

Carey felt the usual amount of gawking as they made their way to the bar. But she felt a tingle from the tips of her toes to all the right places when Owen leaned over and whispered in her ear, "They're staring at you, darling. You're beautiful."

It was difficult to stay focused, but she tried. They both kept their eyes open for Hyde Sutton and Roman Timofeyev. Once found, she and Owen kept a discreet awareness of their locations at all times. It wasn't hard to keep tabs on them during dinner; Hyde and Roman were obviously seated at the same table with Pravdina.

The dinner and the speakers were boring, but sitting next to Owen was not. Even though they'd only just met, their sexual cues could not have been more obvious, and she felt herself floating toward him when he placed his hand under the table and onto her leg and stroked it. She later returned the favor while he was in the midst of a sincere, droll, conversation with the woman seated on his other side. In response, he slid his own hand under the table and found hers, squeezing it with some pressure before carefully removing it from his thigh. He turned back to her as soon as he could and smiled.

Once the dancing began, Carey ached to hold him on the dance floor, but decided that the sooner they got to the purpose of their evening, the sooner they could be alone. They'd spent their time during dinner dutifully charming the society crowd at their table, but they immediately excused themselves to mingle when Roman took leave from his own table.

The duo got up and followed him. Carey, always a voracious drinker, could hold her liquor and party with the best of them, but she was ready to put on a show. Spying Roman at a bar with another man, she and Owen approached. Carey was strung tight and ready to pounce.

Near the bar, Roman watched a very blonde, practically naked woman in a beaded gown walk toward him, saying loudly to her date, "Come on sweetie, just one more drink. I swear to God, just one more, okay? Okay?"

The woman was slightly slurry, but a beautiful sight to behold. Her date rolled his eyes and looked like a man who was very tolerant of a spoiled child in public. He whispered something in her ear and walked off.

"God, what a poo," the woman said loudly to her date's retreating back. She turned quickly and stumbled, catching her balance on Roman's arm. "Oh, sorry, sorry, sorry, sorry, sorry. Man, that doesn't even sound like a word anymore. Does it?" she smiled happily and looked dreamily into Roman's eyes.

Smiling back, Roman helped straighten her up and said, "Hello there. Are you having a nice evening?"

"I wassssss." The woman turned her head and pointed at the last spot her date had been standing and shook her head. She smiled again at Roman. "Would you mind buying me a drink? My date just wandered away to do some business. He said he'd be right back, but who knows. You know?"

"I'd be happy to." Roman smiled.

"Hey, what's your name?" The bombshell rubbed her hand down his arm and looked closely at his jacket sleeve.

"Roman Timofeyev. And you are?" he asked while looking down at her.

"Hi Roman. Is that Russian?" she squinted at him. "It sure sounds Russian. I've never been to Russia though. I'm from California. I'm Carey Carrows. Nice to meet you."

Although always happy to have a beautiful, nearly naked woman on his arm, Roman hadn't known who she was and blinked back his surprise when hearing she was a Carrows. He supposed he'd seen a picture of her, at some point, but was totally thrown by how gorgeous, and obviously very drunk, she was in person.

"It's a pleasure to meet you, too, Ms. Carrows."

"What are you drinking tonight, Mr. Russia. Is it vodka? Oh, I *adore* vodka. Let's do some shots. Yay! Or wait! Do you say *Da*? I'm going to have a vodka shot with a cute Russian! See, the evening wasn't a complete and *total* waste of time."

Roman placed the order and, after receiving their drinks, Carey took his arm and guided him over to a quiet corner to look out into the room and observe the party.

Swaying a bit and holding herself steady on his arm, she said, "Are you having fun, Russia?"

"I am now." He smiled.

"Are you here with a date?"

"No, but you are," he reminded her.

"Oh, my date," she said, throwing her hand to the side to indicate whatever. "He's a nice enough guy, but boooooorrrrrrring. My God, he's like a federal agent or something. Like from the Port Authority, or Homeland Justice Department. Booooorrrrring. I mean he's cute and all, and his dad's like a doctor or something here, so he asked me out to come with him, and here we are! But *government people* just aren't fun! I mean, are they?" she asked like she was truly confused and actually needed an answer.

Roman looked around the crowd. "I haven't had a lot of

experience with government types. Did you say you're from California?"

Carey made like she just noticed the shot of vodka in her hand and put it back. She held out the empty glass for an imaginary waiter to take it from her and grabbed Roman's arm tighter for support.

"Thank you, Russia, for being my friend. Now do you even see where my date went off to. Working the room for big, boring homeland Uncle Sam, no doubt." She held her small, jeweled evening bag above her eyes and scanned the crowd, her head moving fast from side to side, unfocussed.

Roman did the looking for her and straightened a bit when he saw him speaking to Hyde Sutton.

"Do you see him? Where the hell is he?" she slurred impatiently, stomping her foot.

"Yes, he's over there," Roman said, gesturing.

Carey followed his finger and stared, her mouth dropping open. "Oh. My. God. Look. At. Him. He's talking to that big fat pig, Hyde Sutton! What a loser. We hate him, you know. Oh, my God." Suddenly laughing, she added, "I shouldn't be telling you this, but did you know he has a penile implant?" she whispered the last two words behind her hand.

Giggling, she continued, "No shit. Now don't ask me how I know that 'cause I'm not gonna tell you, but I do. I mean he does. He probably needed it to hold up his spine. He's spineless, too, you know. Big fat asshole. We hate him, my sister especially, I mean, and he hates us too. What the hell is Daniel doing talking to him? Let me tell you, that man...what do I care if he hates us? We're Carrows! No, wait, my sister's a Macchi now. Whatever, you know what

I mean. That man, he doesn't care about anyone but himself. Classic narrcisssissst. Look it up! It's in the dictionary. If you look up narrccissssissst, you'll find his picture. Total jackass. Would throw anyone—his wife, his kid, *anyone*—into a pit, give them to the devil if he needed to. Only cares about hisself."

Carey suddenly threw her head and shoulders back. Her ravishing breasts stood at attention as she said, "But you know what! I think his day is coming. He'll get his. Whatever he's got coming, he's got coming. My little birdie over there, my Tweety bird date, he told me that there's something going on with Mr. *Hyde*. So what's he doing talking to him?" she said now, head cocked and confused.

"Hey, Russia, did you want to do another shot? Come on, let's go over to the bar and get another one of those and then you can take me dancing." She beamed at him.

Uncertain about exactly what he'd witnessed, Roman narrowed his eyes at Carey's date as he left Hyde's side and walked back toward them. "I'd be happy to take you dancing, but I'm not sure your date would like that. Here he comes now."

Carey's date looked tightly at her as she began petting the sleeve of Roman's coat. She turned her head and challenged him with a simpering smile.

"Hello, I'm Daniel Parks. Nice to meet you," he said, extending his hand to Roman.

Roman shook his hand and realized they had an awkward situation as Carey wrapped her arm through his and said, "Russia's my new best friend. We didn't miss you. At. All. Did we, Russia?"

"We did not. Would you mind terribly, Mr. Parks if I danced with your lovely date?"

"Actually, something's come up, and it's time for us to go. Carey, I'm terribly sorry, but would you mind if we cut our evening here short?" He looked at his watch and gestured his hand toward the door.

Carey turned her head away from him and pouted.

"Mr.— Russia—was it?" Daniel tilted his head.

"No. Actually it's Roman Timofeyev. Nice to meet you."

Daniel nodded his greeting. "I apologize, Mr. Timofeyev. I'm afraid we need to leave."

Carey slowly, with a lingering sexuality, disengaged herself from Roman. She put her arm through Daniel's, and playfully punched him. "Okay. I guess the evenings over anyway. Let's go. Thanks for the drink, Russia. I've got to say, you were the *funnest* part of my night."

With that, Owen nodded his goodbye to Roman, and he and Carey left the building. Back in their town car, Carey instructed the driver to go to the Carlyle. She pulled out her phone and said, "I'm just going to text Charlotte and Alex." She leaned over so Owen could watch while she typed:

Ball's over, went as planned, don't wait up, I won't be home.

Dropping the phone back into her purse, she raised a perfect eyebrow and smiled. "Did you know that they serve the most de-licious breakfast at the Carlyle, Owen?"

Taking that as really good sign, his heartbeat quickened as he lifted her hand. Stroking the top of it, he turned it over and softly kissed her delicate wrist, while inhaling her glorious scent. "I did not know that, Carey."

Gently dropping her hand, he looked into her perfect face. Her eyes were one big calling card, pulling him, begging him to kiss her, something he'd longed to do all night. He lay his hands gently on either side of her face and kept them there, then rolled them through her soft hair as the warmth of their pulsing chemistry flooded through him, and she gobbled him up with her eyes. His body felt on fire as he, at last, pulled the beauty toward him.

"You," he said, before he leaned into her waiting mouth. The kiss and the entire evening were his tremendous pleasure.

LATER THAT EVENING, Roman ambled over to Hyde. "I met the most interesting woman tonight. Did you see her? Carey Carrows?"

"Yeah, what a drunk. I saw her. I saw you feeling her up too. Not bad tits. I'll give her that."

"I saw you speaking with her date. How do you know him?" Roman casually inquired.

"Oh him?" Hyde said looking blank. "Just a guy. Wants to do a deal. Real estate thing. His dad's a doctor here tonight."

Roman sipped his drink and thought about that.

Chapter 24

Nate Rabideaux, one of the rotating Homeland Security agents assigned to assist the Macchi & Macchi surveillance efforts at Bay Ridge Properties, was bored. Of all the assignments he'd been on, sitting in the back of a van in a parking garage—just in case he was needed to follow a suspected shipment of human cargo—was wearing on him.

The team, originally, had the guys sitting in an old, beat-up, nondescript Ford, but gave that up in case they were noticed. Now, they were holed up in a van parked next to the Ford, but the quiet darkness and inactivity made the evenings challenging. He'd been assigned the 6:00 p.m. to midnight shift. If something was going to go down, there was a good chance it would be during those hours.

His team at Homeland was counting on the private talent from Macchi & Macchi, currently stashed down the street somewhat comfortably in their small nest across from the complex, to manage the actual surveillance. All Nate had to do was to follow the vans if he got the call. Based on the information he'd been given, he knew it could be a dangerous assignment, but that was assuming he ever got the call. So far, it'd been quiet.

Nate yawned, trying to stay awake by playing another game of Sudoku. Hearing small pops from the far-off fireworks display in the harbor, he jumped when his cellphone rang. It was Santa.

"It's happening. Get in the Ford. The boat just tied up. Be ready. If they leave like last time, they'll head north out of the lot. I've got another line open with Josh. He's running downstairs to his car in case they go south. Keep the lines open, I'll give you both the play-by-play.

"It's almost identical as last time. The women were herded off the boat. Goddamit, we should have suspected it was going to happen earlier. I saw a couple vans pull in and not leave. I didn't put it together."

Nate started the Ford, but kept the lights off. He pulled it out of the parking spot, ready to take off.

"Okay guys, women have been loaded into the vans, and the boat is pulling away. Hopefully, we get a name on the thing this time. I couldn't get a clear view through my specs, but we have the footage. Vans coming into view. Guy punching in the numbers for the gate to open. Two vans. Paneled. Dark blue. No signage. Heading out, turning north. Nate! You're up. Good luck, man. Stay safe."

AUGUST

Chapter 25

CLARENCE BEUTZ THOUGHT they had 'em. Sort of. The next morning, he allowed Alex and Michael Macchi to sit in on the task force meeting. It was a courtesy, and Clarence strictly cautioned the two brothers only to watch.

Clarence had been ready to launch a task force after his first meeting with the Macchis, but was told by the higher-ups at Homeland that they needed more evidence and information before the other agencies would commit their resources.

Last night, after watching the latest video sent to him from Santa in the nest, Clarence felt strongly that they had a trafficking pattern. Upset to see that the faces of the women were new and not the same ones from the last boatload, it gave weight to the investigation. The women, once again, looked sick and frightened and were wearing cheap, glittery party dresses. At least one had a black eye.

Clarence had called his boss who, based on this new evidence, greenlighted the plan. It gave Clarence authorization to move ahead at full speed. He called in the members of the team from the FBI, ICE, and Homeland Security for a morning meeting. He didn't involve the local Bay Ridge police because he and the Macchi's weren't sure if they could trust them.

In a large, crowded government conference room with a projection screen at the head, Clarence put up his hand and opened the meeting. "In a moment, I'm going to show you two videos that were obtained by a surveillance team from a private investigations firm. Last month, that firm approached us with information that they'd witnessed what appeared to be a human trafficking event in Bay Ridge. The video convinced me that they were correct in assuming something was wrong, but we needed to see if it was a one-time event or part of a pattern of transfers at a private pier in New York Harbor.

"They have video of a boat, a 59' Carver 570 Voyager, dropping a dozen women at a pier. From a distance they could look like party girls, but up close, you'll see a different picture. The girls were then loaded into two waiting vans and driven away. Unfortunately, after the private security firm witnessed the first transfer, no one was in position to follow them. They obtained the license numbers of the vans, however, and tracked the vehicles to a used car lot in Brooklyn, where they were located the next day, still for-sale, on the lot.

"The second video, recorded last night, features an almost identical performance. The same boat, or the same make of boat, arrives, drops off the women, who are loaded into the back of waiting vans, and driven away. The vans from last night were a different color than the vans from the first event, and as we speak, we're checking with the same used car lot to see if they've been returned."

Clarence looked up from his notes and pointed out into the group. "Last night, Officer Nate Rabideaux from Homeland—Nate, raise your hand—was on the scene in readiness to tail the vans should another transfer happen. Fortunately, he was able to follow them undetected to a warehouse, or a commercial space, in East Williamsburg. From there, he positioned himself to retain surveillance of the property and called for backup. Since then, we have had eyes on the building. More on that later.

"I believe those of you from the Human Trafficking Task force will recognize that the faces of these women and girls represent victims of sex trafficking, but I'll let you be the judge of that. We'll show you feed on both the events. Let's roll the videos."

The room lights were lowered, and representatives of the various agencies watched. There were a few inaudible expressions, and Clarence had the room lights brought up and resumed the debriefing. "Show of hands. Does anyone in this room *not* think these women are victims of human trafficking?"

No one raised their hand.

"All right then. I was asked to gather the opinions from the experts, and I've done that. Now let's get to work to stop the ring and save the women."

He shuffled through his paperwork. "Further facts worth mentioning: Both evenings, there was a harbor event scheduled. New York Bay was filled with pleasure craft, and I believe they think it allows them some cover. Speculating on where the boatload of girls originated from, I can only guess—the Atlantic, but it could have come from a number of places. We just don't know. The private investigation firm also gathered some facts about the transfer site."

Clarence held up the fact sheet they all had in front of them. "The transfer property has a small private pier and is owned by Bay Ridge Properties—address provided on the fact sheet, and is on record, an empty group of derelict warehouses on what could be a valuable piece of real estate. It is owned by the Mercer Investment Group and listed in their portfolio of assets. It is worth noting that the Mercer Investment Group has several investors. The largest, primary, and original owner is Mr. Hyde Sutton of Manhattan. There is no income on record generated from the property. No rent paid and no active business on record at that address. But there are vehicles regularly seen coming and going, many of which are registered to a shell company named ZATO. Any of you heard of it?

Clarence looked around the silent room. "No? Well, we have an unconfirmed source that tells us the company was founded by a Mr. Viktor Timofeyev. Show of hands. Any of you heard of this gentleman?"

Every hand in the room went up.

"It should be noted that last month, before the first known transfer, when Bay Ridge cops needed to investigate a mugging near the Bay Ridge complex, it was difficult to find an English speaker. Most of them spoke Russian."

Clarence laid the fact sheet down on the table in front of him. "Okay then. So unless I am being wildly presumptive, and I don't think I am, Mr. Viktor Timofeyev and his gang of thieves are running a human trafficking ring. Which is the reason we have representatives here from the NYPD Organized Crime Control Bureau.

"Before opening up to questions, I would like to remind every one of you in this room that the element of surprise is the only thing that will save the women in those videos.

If word leaks to the Timofeyev gang before we spring, I guarantee we lose them. So keep it in this room. Also, I want to personally thank the representatives here today from the private security firm who brought this to our attention. They have asked, and I have given them my word, that no one on this task force will leak their names or discuss their role in this investigation."

The team of various agencies began to brainstorm. It took hours to run through the logistical issues and tragically, after several hours of planning, by consensus they agreed they needed more time to pull it together. They decided to hold off raiding the known warehouse and commercial space in East Williamsburg where the last boatload of women was taken.

The task force, led by Clarence, begrudgingly agreed to wait until the next harbor event to conduct the raid. They couldn't be certain that the next shipment would arrive that night, but it was the best guess they had. If the pattern held, there would be another boatload of women arriving at the end of August.

They wanted to round up as many of the players as they could, and Homeland Security and the Port Authority wanted the boat...or at least the driver and men on board to track it back to the gap in their harbor security. In the meantime, the commercial property building in East Williamsburg would be watched by the FBI, and they would gather as much information as possible, which would aid them the night of the takedown. If the women left the property, they would be followed. If they were taken to underground sex clubs, strip clubs, brothels, or stash houses, wherever they went, they would bust all of them simultaneously the night of the raid. Plan B was still in the works.

It was despairingly frustrating to the task force members who were confident that while they organized, the women were being harmed. Heated arguments arose, but warrants were needed and personnel gathered. The night of the next harbor event, replete with fantastic fireworks, could not come soon enough. They had a little under three weeks to prepare.

Meanwhile, Michael and Alex were making their own plans. The fact that the next harbor event coincided with the 52nd Russian Petroushka Ball would be up for discussion in the Hyde war room at Macchi & Macchi later.

Chapter 26

"THE WAIT IS SICKENING," said Alex. "Every day must feel like a hopeless eternity to those women. The fact that we know where some of them are being held is disgraceful."

Michael, his head bent over some papers in the war room said, "I agree, but we both understand why. If they can get 100 bad guys off the street rather than just a few, then it might just be worth it. I know that sounds callous, and you know I don't mean it that way, but our hands are tied. At least it gives us time to meet with the other agencies about supporting the victims after they're rescued. How's Charlotte doing?"

Alex said, "She just closed on the beach house in Mantoloking. She's down there today with a crew getting it set up. Clarence greased the wheels and got it fast-tracked as a temporary residential placement center. With a full-time, credentialed staff, it can house up to ten of the victims."

Alex picked up a pile of paperwork. With Karla Fernandez at Sutton Tower, everyone had been working overtime to keep up with the meetings they'd taken from various agencies and support groups. He picked a fact sheet out of the stack and walked over to the board and to the enlarged images of the victims from the boats. He tacked up the copy.

"It's going to be a long journey for them, physically and mentally. There'll be legal issues, immigration issues. Most of them will probably suffer from PTSD, and the trauma services are stretched incredibly thin. It's messed up that after they're found, they're usually farmed out to domestic violence shelters, mental health facilities, hotels, even homeless shelters. At least we know that ten of them will have a stable place to stay. But God knows what kind of shape they'll be in. Charlotte's got a bank of translators ready."

Michael rocked in his chair, listening. "It's great that you're doing that, Alex. Remind yourself that we do what we can."

Alex walked down the war board and stopped at Hyde's picture. He tried clearing the bad taste in his mouth as he stared at the putrid face. In the picture, Hyde's mouth was twisted into a sneer, and his eyes were closed. It was a blowup from the *Post*, and Karla had drawn a toothbrush mustache on it. "Which brings us back to Mr. Hyde, who allowed all this to happen in the first place.

"We know that both Roman Timofeyev and Hyde will be attending the Petroushka Ball. Nothing about Viktor—but Hyde, Pravdina, and Roman have confirmed attendance, so we know where they'll be the night of the raid. Assuming it happens."

Alex picked up some paperwork on the Petroushka Ball being held this year at the Plaza, the same place as the Sloan Kettering thing. "I don't think any of us need to attend. The less Roman Timofeyev sees us or thinks about the Macchis or Carrows, the better. Carey and Owen planted the first seed of mistrust into Roman's ear. That one couldn't have gone better.

"Roman Timofeyev believes Owen works for the government, and he saw him speaking with Hyde. So what we need to do now is reinforce that scenario. We need pictures of Owen and Hyde meeting again, ready to send to Mr. Timofeyev when the shit hits the fan."

Michael said, "I was thinking we might get the biggest bang for our buck if Owen could be seen with Hyde the actual night of the ball, before Hyde and Pravdina leave Sutton Tower. Maybe in the lobby. That way, if we send Roman a picture of his good friend Hyde hugging it out with a government official before his operation blows up, he'll be able to recognize what they were wearing, and time stamp it. Hyde's fashion is outrageous. God knows what he'll be wearing that night, which goes for Pravdina as well. Roman will take one look at the picture and realize that Hyde met with Homeland Security the night of the raid."

Alex made a note of the potential meeting under the timeline for the night of the raid. "I like it. You think it will be enough?"

"No. We're going to need more. We'll keep the tapes rolling in the penthouse. Maybe we'll get something from Hyde's mouth after the police come to get him."

Alex capped the pen. "He's not going to say anything to the police. He'll let his lawyer do all the talking."

"That's correct. But when he's *home alone*, he's going to do plenty of talking. Screaming will be more like it. So we need to give him something to scream about. What if we have Owen meet with Hyde in the lobby on the night of the ball, and have him shoot a little paranoia into Hyde's relationship with the Russians. Let's make the man a tiny bit suspicious when he's around his good pal Roman."

"That could work." Alex said and took his seat. He liked where this was going.

Michael asked, "Did Clarence say he would loan us a Homeland Security jacket for the night of the raid?"

"He's been noncommittal. He wants to know what we intend to do with it." Alex smirked. "I mean, we could have one made if we wanted to; he must know that."

"Then tell him we just need to have one of our employees wear it for a photo op at the crime scene at the hostage site. He'll put it on, we'll take a few pictures of him around the action along with the Feds, and then we'll give the jacket back."

Alex nodded. "Tell Clarence I expect him to make it happen. Tell him that the night of the raid, we want to be kept in the loop. By him and him alone. At some point, when the shooting stops, we'll be sending one of our guys over to borrow his jacket and take his picture in it. Then we'll disappear, and the photos will never surface. I want this done, Michael."

Michael shrugged. "I think he'll be agreeable."

"Should we worry about the danger we're putting Owen in?"

"If the Timofeyev's think Owen's a cop, and of course, they think his name is Daniel Parks—which won't come up in any data base—they won't be able to find him. Not that they would go after a cop. There will be too many of them, and Daniel Parks is just one in a pack. I think it's more likely Hyde would look for him."

"I'm not worried about Hyde," said Alex.

"What about the other kind of danger we've exposed Owen to."

"What's that?" Alex cocked his head.

"To your sister-in-law, Carey. They've been 'keeping company' since Sloan Kettering. Ever think there's not real danger there?"

Alex smirked, but couldn't stop himself from smiling. "First our brother Nick, and now the dashing Owen Kai. You know I have no control of her, right?"

"I know, I'm only joking. I'm sure Owen's perfectly safe. He's a big boy and knows what he's doing."

Alex smiled. "He may have met his match."

Michael stared at the ceiling. "Owen Kai Carrows. It has a lovely ring to it."

"It can't go that far."

Michael shrugged, "Crazier things have happened, and from the looks of things, Owen's finally fallen hard."

"But *Carey* may not have, and frankly, the less I know the better. Call the boy and pull him away from his activities. We need to bring him up to speed," said Alex.

"I believe he's been staying at the Carlyle since the night you introduced them."

"This is not my fault, Michael. And I warned him, okay?"

Michael smiled. "I'm just saying... Owen always did know how to catch the big wave."

Chapter 27

THE PETROUSHKA BALL was celebrating its fifty-two-year anniversary. Supporting the Russian Children's Welfare Society's charitable programs, such as educational scholarships for orphans, medical treatment for children with severe facial deformities, and other rehabilitation programs, it was a glamorous annual event.

That evening, Karla Fernandez, three floors below the Sutton Penthouse suite, poured herself a large glass of wine as she listened in to the conversations in Hyde Sutton's study.

"What did I tell you and that little bitch, Pravdina? No bullshit! You need to be classy. *Classy* with a capital C! You can't wear that nothing, nobody designer! Everyone needs to know that you're wearing a dress from a *haute couture* line, a name they'll remember. People are going to *ask you* what you're wearing! I don't give a shit what fucking pet project or pet designer that little stylist bitch wants you to wear, you're wearing the Valentino. End of discussion. You already had your highlights done to accent the red in the dress, so no more arguing. Just go put it on, and it better be ready and altered for you. No shit, Prav. I'll fire that pansy-assed fruit if it's not perfect! This is the last time I give into you and let you keep that flaming queen on staff if you don't come back in here looking like a goddamn *ten*."

Screaming down the hallway, "Perfect, Pravdina! Think perfect! And don't forget the fucking gloves!"

Karla slugged back the alcohol as she watched Hyde, now alone in his office, walk over to his enormous mirror and prance back and forth, patting his stomach and admiring himself. "That stupid bitch," he said to his reflection. "She better watch her fucking step. You could probably do better, my man. Probably. No one would turn you away. The women in Russia were drooling over you. Think about all the wild shit they let you do to them. You could have your fucking pick of good-looking ass over there."

Karla picked up the phone and called Owen, who had been waiting. "Now. Call now. Perfect time. She's getting into her dress, and they'll probably be leaving in the next ten minutes."

Owen, already waiting in the lobby of Sutton Tower, did just that.

Hyde answered. "Yeah."

"Mr. Sutton? I'm sorry to disturb you, sir. Perhaps you remember me? Daniel Parks, Homeland Security?"

Karla watched Hyde throw his head back and roll his eyes.

"Yeah. What can I do for you?"

"It's what I can do for you, Mr. Sutton. Listen, I'm near Sutton Tower, just pulling up, as a matter of fact, and I was wondering if I could pop up for a quick word with you? Are you available this evening?"

"No. I'm going out."

"All I need is one minute. Can I meet you in the lobby on your way out?"

"What is it? Can't you tell me over the phone?" Hyde resumed looking at himself in the mirror.

"I'd rather not."

"All right. Fine. One minute. In the lobby. We'll be down in five minutes," he said and hung up.

"What the fuck now?" Hyde asked his reflection. "I can't do his goddamned job for him too. I've got my own life to live. Do your own fucking job, Mr. Parks!" Hyde yelled at his dead phone then tucked it into his pocket.

Karla called Owen. "They're leaving. He's pissed. You ready?"

"No worries. Josh is in place. We'll send you the pictures."

HYDE SUTTON GOT OFF the elevator with the ever-glamorous Pravdina, wearing her red Valentino from the designer's volcano line. With matching silk gloves and her hair beautifully colored to enhance the red tones in the gown, she was stunning, but she didn't look happy about it.

Owen rushed over to Hyde and grabbed his hand. He smiled broadly and used the other hand to pat him on the back. "Mr. Sutton, thank you for giving me a moment of your time. I'm so grateful."

Hyde stopped and looked at him. "Well what is it? And by the way, what in the hell were you doing at the Sloan Kettering gala with that drunk Carey Carrows?"

Owen put his hand over his heart and shook his head in a humble gesture. "That's exactly why I wanted to see you sir. My boss heard that you might not approve of that relationship, and he thought it would be a good idea to let you know that we are totally and completely supportive of you. I would never dream, not in a million years, of letting you think otherwise. We didn't want to muddy the communication lines between us. As a matter of fact," Owen gently steered Hyde two feet away from his wife and lowered his voice. "As a matter of fact, sir, I also thought you deserved a small heads up, as a show of good faith from our agency, that there might...might possibly be a forthcoming investigation into one of your business partners." Owen leaned over and whispered in Hyde's ear, "Roman Timofeyev. Nothing too serious, mind you, but from one patriotic organization to another, well, there it is. But remember, please don't mention it to anyone else, sir."

Owen grabbed Hyde's hand and pumped it, saying with louder enthusiasm, "Thank you, Mr. Sutton, for your time and your understanding on that Carrows' situation that might have been misconstrued and for your support of our national defense. Let me give you my card, and if there is anything you need to discuss later, just give me call."

Hyde took the card and looked at it. All it contained was the name Daniel Parks and a cell number. He put it in his pocket and turned to Pravdina, who waited patiently like she was on her way to a funeral.

"Yeah, right."

At that, Hyde turned to leave the building. Pravdina moped and followed several paces behind him.

Chapter 28

"DAMN, IT LOOKS GOOD, Owen!" Karla said when she got the images. "Josh did a great job. It looks like you're thanking the shit out of him for something. The whispering looks confidential like you're best friends in some conspiracy. Well done."

"I aim to please. I hope Hyde does something with the paranoia I threw his way. You don't think he'd say anything to alert them tonight, do you?"

"Not a chance," said Karla.

"God, that would be tragic. So let's set our watch. The fireworks start sometime after 9:30 and if history is an indicator, the boat should pull up to the pier around 10:00. The women will unload and get into the waiting vans. Santa will alert everyone and videotape it. They'll be in place to follow them in case they go elsewhere, but if they pull up to the building in East Williamsburg, then it's a green-light go...all over the city and in the harbor. God willing this nightmare will be over soon."

"God willing the women won't be hurt. I mean, any more than they've already been," said Karla.

"I know what you mean."

IT HAPPENED. When the two vans loaded with the women were blocks away from the commercial space in East Williamsburg, the signal was given, and all systems were go. Cops with sirens came from every direction and blocked the vans on the street. Guns were drawn, and overhead, a helicopter lit up the action. The men in the vehicles were taken without gunfire, and the vans' back doors were thrown open to the faces of nearly hysterical women.

In the harbor, the FBI, aboard a Coast Guard cutter, gave chase and boarded without incident the same 59' Carver 570 voyager that had made all three drops at the warehouse and arrested the men. After a short, violent interrogation, the cops realized the men were not going to speak, but based on the previous videos, they had located the boat and installed a tracking device earlier that week. Nearly twelve miles out in the Atlantic, the Coast Guard and Homeland Security were also boarding a large merchant vessel from the Great Atlantic Line, bearing a house flag from India. It would take many months of international cooperative investigations to unravel the chain of custody and persons involved in the human-tracking scheme.

The Bay Ridge Properties complex was seized and only one man with weapons was arrested at that site. They also found boxes of various medical equipment and merchandise that belonged to a company named Med Source. It would take some time for the FBI to uncover whether illegal trade or business was taking place in the complex...other than human smuggling, of course.

Across Manhattan and the outer boroughs, nearly half a dozen sex clubs and bars where women were being used as sex slaves were closed and the owners and customers arrested.

The biggest tragedy, however, took place at the East Williamsburg commercial building. SWAT and teams from the FBI, ICE, and Homeland Security raided the building, firing shots and killing several well-armed men who resisted. After securing the property, the authorities were horrified to find at least six women in various states of consciousness, living in filth and requiring hospitalization. It was not immediately clear if they had been drugged, starved and were ill or traumatized beyond redemption, but they were quickly triaged and left in ambulances.

Over the course of the evening, Clarence Beutz continually notified Alex about what they'd found. Keeping his word—but not at all happy about it—while the activity around the scene at the warehouse was at its peak, he let Owen into the area and handed him an extra Homeland Security jacket. Owen moved around the scene with Clarence, his head posed in various directions until Josh texted him that he had enough. Owen gave the jacket back and left the scene.

Female police officers assisted the emotional and confused women from the vans and transported them to a local hospital for treatment and to be interviewed. The police needed Russian and Ukrainian translators to accomplish it. One by one, they gathered their names and addresses, their sad stories, and their family contacts.

Social workers assessed the situation and felt that the ten women newly arrived that evening from the vans had formed a survivor's group and should stay together while the wheels of the system decided how to manage the various problems. Most of them were capable and could leave the hospital by the next day; a luxury bus was waiting for them at the hospital exit to take them to their temporary residential placement center. Nine women, two translators, and one social worker boarded the bus for the one hour and forty-minute drive to Mantoloking, NJ.

One of the wealthiest communities in New Jersey, population 296, Mantoloking is located on part of New Jersey's Gold Coast with miles of pristine white sandy beaches. After the bus left Manhattan traffic and worked its way through the suburbs to the small township, the passengers grew quiet as they gazed at the mansions overlooking the ocean. Pulling up to a huge beachfront property, they were escorted off the bus into their new home.

The house featured six large bedrooms, each with single beds to accommodate as many people as possible. Each bedroom was painted in white or soft hues of blue and green pastels. The bedrooms were accented with homey quilts and antique headboards. The large cozy great room with exposed beams overlooked a wraparound porch with rocking chairs that faced their private beach and pool. The women found the bathrooms stocked with toiletries and the closets and drawers with comfortable clothing in a variety of sizes. A woman in the kitchen was quietly laying out plates and preparing their lunch.

The translators told them to make themselves at home and take the day to rest. They would be staying with the women in the one of the rooms. The house would be crowded, but none of them seemed to mind. All of the women were eager to bathe or shower, and the seven bathrooms were busy as they took turns bathing and crying and felt some of the adrenaline leave their exhausted bodies.

Over the course of the next few days, a revolving door of appointments was set for each of them with various legal, medical, and social services. The women would also be a great help to one another, comforting and intimately understanding what they were all experiencing. The day staff would see to their various needs, setting up umbrellas on the beach and encouraging them to spend part of each day outdoors.

It wasn't paradise, not in the way that it should have been, but it was life. Their life coming back into focus, and each of them finding a path toward wanting to live it.

Curled in a ball on her bed looking out toward the ocean, Freya Brown wasn't sure if she even wanted that anymore.

Chapter 29

THE SHIT HIT THE FAN. The night after the raid and the Petroushka Ball, Roman Timofeyev ran to open the front door of his house in Brooklyn as his dad entered. Viktor had a key and hadn't waited for Roman to arrive. Roman saw the sour, bitter sneer on his father's face and said, "Dad. Hey. Let's go to the safe room."

The safe room was a specially designed space in the basement that was protected from electronic eavesdropping equipment. Soundproof, they could speak freely. Sometimes, the room was used for other purposes.

Viktor entered the space and looked around at the sparse furnishings then sat awkwardly in an uncomfortable wooden chair. "Did you enjoy yourself last night at ball," he asked with a menacing tone.

Roman knew that when his father was angry, nothing he could do would temper it. Changing the subject, he tucked his blond hair behind his ears and said, "What happened?"

"We had problems with shipment. Operation in East Williamsburg was shut down. Some of men are dead; rest have been arrested. Bay Ridge shut down. More arrests. Maybe seven arrested. I don't know. Maybe more. Maybe some got away. Two dead, Andy and Carl. That I heard. Lawyers on move. Working on bail to get them out. It is mess."

Roman was no fool. He knew that the pier at Bay Ridge was being used to smuggle unwilling women into the country. He knew they were being held prisoner and turned into sex slaves in East Williamsburg. He knew, but he was never an active participant in that part of the organization. Viktor wanted to protect him from the lucrative illegal activities that financed their legitimate investments. Physically, at least.

Roman realized this was really bad news, but he had no clue what his father would do next. "So what happens now?"

Viktor absentmindedly turned a gold ring on his pinky finger, which he did a lot when he was angry and thinking. "We wait and see. Lawyers. They make much money on this."

Roman thought about pulling out a chair and sitting but decided against it. He stood at attention. "Do you think they'll come after us?"

"I don't know, but I think they will question me. They love to harass me, so I expect this. For you? I don't know. You are partner in Bay Ridge. Partner in Mercer Investments. Will they investigate all partners? How many are there? How many Wall Street big shots have money in Mercer?"

Roman answered, "Not many. Three. Do you think the guys will talk? We're the only ones using the warehouse in Bay Ridge, not the other partners. By now, the cops know that Med Source does business over there."

"I'm not so worried about this. No laws are broken using warehouse. Maybe tax issues. The boat, the women..." He shrugged, adding, "Men know consequences for speaking. Their families will die or worse. This is known. I think they say nothing. Yet. We will see. In meantime, maybe you should take vacation? Go to Prague. Work on development? Or St. Petersburg?"

Roman felt jumpy and a little nauseous. The night before, after hearing about the raids, he knew they were in trouble. The close connection and his partnership involvement with Mercer and the Bay Ridge pier put him too close to the bull's-eye. After he'd become a partner in Mercer—which had been, primarily, to solidify his relationship with Hyde Sutton and several other high rollers—his father had taken a look at the portfolio and discovered the unused pier in Bay Ridge. It was too tempting for Viktor and he'd told Roman to ask Hyde for permission to use the complex for storage of their inventories from their legitimate medical supply business, Med Source. Hyde had agreed, and the Timofeyev gang grabbed the opportunity to use the pier for their other lucrative imports from Europe.

Now that the pier's use had been discovered, he and his father were trying to determine who might have blown their cover. If it was an inside job from someone who was part of the Timofeyev family, then they were idiots. So someone from outside? A snitch?

"I'm not sure where we'll stand on the development deals with Hyde Sutton now," Roman said carefully. "He's going to be pissed that the pier at Bay Ridge was being used as a drop-off. He'll be pissed at me, personally, for asking to use it, and what if he tells the cops? He's gotta tell them, right? Also, something else has been bothering me; I didn't think much about it at the time, but now things are different."

Viktor stared up at him, his eyes hungry, and waited. Roman shuffled his feet. "At the Sloan Kettering Ball, I saw Hyde talking to a government agent."

His father's face darkened, and Roman could visually see his blood pressure rising. "What part of government?"

"I'm not really sure. I only found out the guy was an agent because I happened to talk to his drunk date, who told me the guy works for Homeland Security. But then she backtracked and said Port Authority or the Justice Department. Frankly, she sounded like she wasn't sure."

"Do you think Hyde is working with government?" Viktor growled.

"I don't know, but I don't think we can totally trust him. He's not part of the family, and he doesn't understand the way we do business. I think, if he were put in a corner, he'd do whatever he needed to get out. I'm not saying he will, but he's not going to take the blame for any of this without a fight, and I know he'll point fingers away from himself."

Viktor glared at him with disbelief. "What about business? Money is on table. He would walk away?"

"No. I don't know about that. He might want to pull out, which would leave us vulnerable, but he can't do it legally without going through a shitload of crap. Maybe he'd use this situation, though, you know, as an excuse. We might end up having to renegotiate the deals with the oligarchs too. They'll hear about this, and if Hyde tries to pull out, you know they'll use it against us. I'm pretty sure they'll stay in bed with us—I mean the developments will be amazing—but they may try to force us out and work with Hyde directly. Or Hyde could. We could potentially lose a lot on this."

"So we need to see what Mr. Badass Sutton's balls tell him to do. Either way, if he is rat or tries to cross us, he is dead."

Roman knew that was a fact, but he wondered if Hyde Sutton had any idea that his days might be numbered.

Chapter 30

THE NUMBER OF law enforcement agencies who had worked together to pull off the raids was nothing compared with the legal clusterfuck the fallout created. The Department of Defense, Department of Transportation, U.S. Customs and Border Protection, DOJ, Homeland Security, FBI, Coast Guard, and the NYC police and its agencies each had a role to play in the prosecution of the ring. Fortunately, they had some time to prepare before the raids, and Homeland Security was given command.

Charges were being drawn up, and the various members of the Timofeyev gang were not, as Viktor predicted, talking. Clarence Beutz, as head of the operation, was trying to work his way up the ladder to those responsible and hit the big guys. A part of that investigation was interviewing the owners of the Bay Ridge Properties and all of the Mercer Investment Group partners. Hyde Sutton was at the top of the list.

Clarence and several other members of the team walked

into Sutton Tower, unannounced and used their credentials to get to Hyde's office. Flashing a badge at the young blonde admin outside Hyde's door she said he was in an important meeting and couldn't be disturbed.

Clarence shrugged and brushed past her. "We're going in." He and his entourage pushed through the door and into the inner sanctum—the center of the hive, as the admin shouted, "You can't go in there!"

They came to a halt taking in the unexpected scene. Hyde was lying on a massage table, a small towel covering his privates, a young woman in an outfit not suitable for public with her breasts mostly exposed and cinched together turned toward them holding a bottle of oil.

"What the fuck?" Hyde exploded, sitting up. The towel slipped and he grabbed it, positioning it back in place, but not before revealing the gold condom.

Clarence didn't know whether to feel amused or repulsed by the scene, but went into action and held up his badge. "Clarence Beutz. Homeland Security. We're here to question you about your pier and warehouse in Bay Ridge."

"Buts? Get the fuck out of here!" Hyde yelled at them.

Clarence glanced to a sofa near the wall, having not spied a gentleman seated there with white hair and large round heavy glasses. He recognized the guy as a political operative from Florida who had been making the news for stirring up trouble outside a recent democratic convention. The guy dressed as flamboyantly as Hyde usually did and appeared quite amused by the new arrivals.

"We're not leaving until we get some answers."

Hyde jumped off the table, barely holding the cloth in position. "I'm not talking to you without a lawyer. You're trespassing. I'll call security and have you thrown out."

Clarence eyeballed the masseuse who had run over to the man on the couch and was whispering in his ear. He didn't know what was happening, but Hyde was naked. No one was prepared to conduct an interview under these circumstances. It was enough that they'd delivered the seriousness of their request. He took a card out of his pocket and handed it to the blushing admin. "Tomorrow morning; 9:00 a.m. at this address at the Department of Homeland Security. You show up with your lawyer, or we'll come back, arrest you, and perp walk you out of the building. Naked as a jaybird or not."

The next day, Hyde, still incredibly angry, showed up with his lawyers for the acrimonious interview. Hyde may have been instructed to say nothing unless directed, but he opened his mouth as soon as he entered the room and bellowed, "So are you fucktards harassing all the partners in Mercer or just picking on me? Because this is bullshit, and you know it."

Hyde's lawyer jumped in to remind Hyde not to answer any questions. Clarence's eyes widened as Hyde shouted at his lawyer. "Shut up, Thad!"

As grueling and difficult as the meeting turned out to be, by the end, the cops learned very little. Hyde declared to have no knowledge of the pier being used for any particular purpose, let alone for human trafficking, but admitted he had allowed one of his partners to use the site as a temporary warehouse facility, as a personal favor, since it essentially sat vacant.

The investigators moved on and met with the other partners in Mercer, who also claimed no knowledge about how the property was used. That held true until they interviewed Roman Timofeyev. A different kind of evil, dressed in a much prettier package.

The tall, blonde, lean, and elegantly dressed Roman Timofeyev looked like he belonged on a catwalk rather than in the mob. Not a tat in sight and unlike his father in so many ways, his squared shoulders and chin ran parallel to the straight brows over his squinty blue eyes. He also had one of the best lawyers in the city representing him and the lawyer did all of the talking. His client acknowledged that they were using the Bay Ridge Properties complex as a warehouse for his medical supply business, Med Source, but Roman was not a part of the day-to-day operations or knew anything else relevant. Law enforcement would need to prove any wrongdoing.

Lastly, and with much excitement, the team managed to produce the legendary Viktor Timofeyev. His son's lawyer appeared again, and once more declared no knowledge of anything about anything. Viktor himself, never spoke, no matter how much they tried to provoke him. Law enforcement would need to prove it.

Chapter 31

HYDE SUTTON MAY NOT have been spoken much about anything relevant during his meeting with Homeland Security, but he had plenty to say to his lawyer that evening while Karla Fernandez, three floors below, listened.

"They're fucking pond scum! Look what they did to me! Suddenly, I'm in front of the goddamned *police* talking about human trafficking? This could hurt me! If that happens, I'm going to sue the pants off of them. Right, Thad?"

Karla once again recognized Hyde was conducting a rhetorical conversation with his lawyer.

"What do you think? Should I stick with these assholes? St. Petersburg, I gotta say, it was looking good. Real Good. I think the money's going to be huge on this one. But the hell? If this gets out, it could do some damage. Maybe not with the other investors or the big-money people, but with the average Joe. But now that I think about it, what do I care what they think about me, right? I'm a legend. I'm too big to fail. Everyone knows that. Everyone. You just do your job and make sure those asshole cops know to keep a lid on this. If they give the press my name, then we sue. Homeland Security Department, my ass. They can't touch me. Brush up on your slander and libel laws, pal, just in case. We need to be ready for them."

And on it went. Karla called Alex and told him, in real time, what was happening.

"Thanks, Karla, I'll take it from here."

Alex got on the burner phone with his special source at the *New York Post*. The *Post* didn't know who he was, but Alex had been throwing credible tips to the same reporter, Ben Quick, for years. They had a mutually beneficial relationship.

"Hey, Quick, I'm going to send you some images. I've got Hyde Sutton and his lawyers going into the office of Homeland Security. They were forced to come in and be interviewed about their intimate knowledge about the human-trafficking bust in East Williamsburg. Seems the pier where the women were brought ashore onto U.S. soil belongs to Mr. Sutton and his partner, Roman Timofeyev. That's Timofeyev, son of Viktor 'The Arm' Timofeyev, Russian mob boss. You'd be safe to say that they were partners. Check out the owners of Mercer Investment Group. If I were you, I'd want to know exactly how deep Hyde Sutton was involved. He's in big trouble with the Feds."

Thanks to the surveillance, Macchi & Macchi had known when Hyde was giving his interview with the cops. They had a photographer there to capture it. Alex sent it to Ben Quick at the *Post*.

BEN QUICK WAS aptly named as he ran down the hall to meet with his editor. "The Button Man," as Alex was known by Ben, had been an invaluable source who had never let them down. After showing his editor the images of Hyde and his attorneys entering the lower Manhattan office of Homeland Security, Ben wanted to know if he could run with the story.

The editor was uncertain how to proceed and brought in the lawyers. After more round-robin conferences and based on the fact that Quick had confirmed Hyde Sutton and Roman Timofeyev were actually partners in Mercer Investment Group, which also owned Bay Ridge Properties, they decided it would be safe to print. The next morning, the headline in the *New York Post*, in its largest, screaming-bold font read:

MR. HYDE! TELL US WHAT YOU KNOW!

And the story broke.

Chapter 32

RIDING IN THE BACK of the van on the night of her rescue, Freya thought her heart would explode when she heard the sirens and saw the police lights flashing. She didn't know if her captors would kill them all or if they would be rescued only to face some other hell. She didn't trust any of it. The other women felt the same way and were hysterical when their captors were taken out of the van at gunpoint; the back doors were thrown open with guns pointed at them too. One by one, the women were taken out of the van and frisked. Someone then threw a blanket around her shoulders and guided her to a curb.

"Do you speak English," were the first words she heard, and somewhere inside of her, she cracked. Her mind was sensing that the scene around her was a rescue. She had no idea where she was and hardly believed the reality she was experiencing was real. Overcome, a policewoman held her and, eventually, walked her to an ambulance where she held the hand of another one of the girls on the way to a hospital. Crazy, frenetic activity engulfed her as the gurneys carrying the women—her companions from hell—came together. Doctors and nurses were asking them many questions, and Freya was one of the few who could speak English. It was primarily up to her to explain what had happened to the police, the doctors, and everyone else.

Between bursts of tears and furious shaking, she was able to piece together the ordeal for them and finally, finally, she was calm enough to make a phone call to her parents. A very kind woman brought her into a quiet room, handed her a phone, and held her hand as Freya violently trembled and entered her parent's number. Although to her, it had seemed like an eternity, when she'd been told the date, she realized that she had only been gone for three weeks. Long enough, of course, for her parents to be alerted to her abduction, and long enough for them to be horribly traumatized as well.

The sound of her loving mother's voice, whom she had wished for so desperately while being bound and tortured, was suddenly there. Freya only managed to say the word, "Mummy," before breaking into tears. Her mother was frantic to confirm that it was her beloved daughter on the phone, and Freya understood it was vital to control herself and let her know that she was all right, had been rescued, and was in New York. A mix of relief, joy, desperation, and confusion overwhelmed them within moments. They stayed on the phone for some time before the social worked asked to speak with them.

She took over and confirmed to the Brown family that Freya was being cared for at a New York City hospital and was safe. She and some of the other victims would be transferred shortly to a residential placement center. Freya could call them again once she was settled. They could sort through the next steps at that time, but the worst was behind them, and she assured them that Freya was now safe.

Nine of the women from her boat, including her friend, Tina, were deemed medically safe to leave the hospital and were taken by bus to the home she was staying in now. A palace on a beach, for heaven's sake, in New Jersey, America.

Upon arrival they'd all been given their own cell phones, and once in her room, she called her parents to give them the number. They immediately wanted to come to the United States to be with her, but Freya knew it would be a hardship for them to come. She also explained that there were legal considerations, and she had to meet with more police and lawyers who would help to get her home. There were passport and visa applications that needed to be obtained, and apparently, that would take some time. Freya advised them to come later after she learned more. In the meantime, her parents sent what documentation they could to her at the house. All they and Freya could do was wait for the legal process to unfold and set her free.

That was one piece. The other was the shattered bits of her heart and soul. She knew she was safe. She kept telling herself that she was safe. Just that day, she'd had her first meeting with her attorney, and during the course of the interview, she felt a normalcy, a return of some control along with a bit of her strength and power. But then she went out to the beach and began crying again. She didn't know what to think and she feared she would never be the same Freya Brown again. So who was she now?

During the interview with her lawyer, who was arranging a T Visa, or temporary visa, to legally allow her presence in the United States, and obtain documents to travel home, she'd started asking questions: "Are there other victims in another beach house nearby?"

Her lawyer, a kind woman by the name of something Walker, shook her head. "No. As a matter of fact, I've never seen a nicer residential placement center. Anywhere. I won't insult you by saying that you're lucky, Freya, but it's my understanding that you and the other women are being housed by a philanthropic organization. Something very new. I've never heard of this place, but I have to tell you that it's light years away from some of the other treatment facilities I've seen. The others are sterile, more governmental, and impersonal—a bit more crowded, you know. This is an actual home that's been made over for you and the other survivors to help you transition after what you've gone through."

"Is it the Red Cross?"

"No. I have the name somewhere, but I'm not familiar with the group. If you'd like, I could get the name for you."

"Yes. Please."

Freya didn't know what she would do with the name of the organization, but she didn't want to seem rude.

Each day the women came together for group counseling in the living room. Other than the initial interview with the police and the lawyers, who were now a part of their day, they were mostly left to their own devices and used the home and the beach and the phones to begin again and make their plans for returning home. They were told to be patient, that it would take some time, but in the meantime, if there was anything, anything at all that they needed, all the they needed to do was ask.

Freya didn't know what to ask for, but she wished her mum were with her now, holding her hand. But she didn't think that would happen any time soon. She'd lied bitterly to her parents that she was doing okay and they should stay home, but she was trying to be strong for all of them.

It was powerful to see images of the rescue and shocking to see pictures of her captors in the newspapers. She read with horror about the conditions of women who were found at their destination and realized that she had escaped in the nick of time. God knows what fate they had been saving for her and Tina by not raping them, but she knew that she had come very close to a new hell. The other women on her boat had not been as lucky. And while Freya and the others were forced to watch all the multiple rapes, she still couldn't imagine what it would take for them to heal.

Lucky. Lucky. She thought about that word and tried to make it her own. She didn't feel lucky, but then there were degrees of hell, and she'd been spared many of them. Another thing she felt—and could feel more acutely—was anger. She was becoming extremely angry, and if she believed the counselors, that was a good thing; it meant she was a fighter and could recover. She wasn't sure about that, but when she saw pictures of the arrested abductors, her anger felt alive and intensely physical.

THAT NIGHT IN BED she Skyped with her parents, telling them about her day and that she was safe in her own room. She wanted to make them feel better, so she'd sent them pictures of her room, the house, and the beach. They could share in her recovery experience by visualizing where she was staying. And it had helped...a little. Her mother asked, "And are you lying on your bed, angel, and can ye hear the ocean waves?"

"I can, Mummy. They sound nice. We have very tight

security here and a curfew, so everyone is in the house, and the security system is on. Some of the girls are watching TV and some are bathing. The house has incredible tubs, really big ones with all these bath salts and lotions to choose from. So it smells nice too."

"We love you, Freya," said her da. "And remember, just tell us when, and we'll come right away. In the meantime, know that we're holding you here," and he pointed to his heart.

After hanging up, Freya curled in a ball and wept yet again; she missed them so much. Later, one of the ladies who worked in the house stopped in and asked about her day. Freya was beginning to hate herself for all of her tears, especially when around the other women who had suffered more than she had. So she tried to pull it together and said, "Good. Good. I just miss me parents so much. I wish I could see them, is all."

The woman nodded and told her to stay strong and that she would see them soon. Freya wasn't so sure about that. They weren't just oceans away, but worlds now. She would never, ever again be their little innocent girl, no matter how many times they reminded her of that and called her an angel. It broke her heart.

Sarah, who was a social worker and the housemother, left Freya's room and heard the sobbing resume the moment she closed the door. Decision made, she went downstairs and picked up her cell. She was the only person in the house who knew how to reach the actual owner and the face behind the charitable organization attached to it.

"Charlotte, this is Sarah. You asked me to call if there was anything you could do, and I think there is. One of the women here, well, she's a girl, really; her name is Freya. She was abducted near her university in St. Petersburg, Russia, where she was studying for a semester. She's actually from Glasgow, Scotland, and speaks English, so I've been able to talk to her more than others and know her better. You know the legal process is going to take some time; in fact, the police are coming out here in a few days with the district attorney to gauge their reactions to becoming witnesses against their abductors. It's going to be very emotional, and I expect some confusion and fear and some setbacks too. But Freya, she's just so sad and misses her mum and dad.

"It's my understanding that she doesn't want them to travel to her yet because they can only afford to come over once, and she doesn't know how long she'll be tied up here. Frankly, neither do I, and if the district attorney is looking for women to testify in court, then this could all be purposefully delayed and take a really long time. You asked me to call if there was anything you could do, and I think Freya, who is afraid to ask for too much, would benefit greatly in her recovery if she could see her parents sooner than later. What do you think?"

"Can you give me their names and numbers, Sarah? I'll give them a call tonight and have them on the next flight over if they can come."

"Oh, Charlotte, that would be wonderful. I'm sure the other women, at least some of them, would like to see their families too, but I just haven't been able to communicate with them like I can with Freya. I really think it will help her."

"I should have thought of it earlier. I guess I just didn't understand how long this process was going to take. I'll call them now."

Chapter 33

HYDE WAS WILD the night the news broke in the *Post*. Karla laid her head in her arms as the hysteria escalated three floors above her.

On the phone with Thad, Hyde was screaming: "...their heads on a fucking platter! You hear me! The editors. Dead. The writer. Dead. Clarence Beutz, Homeland Security! Dead. He leaked this! It had to be him. One of them. And if he's the man, if he's in charge, he's dead."

"Hyde! You can't talk like that!" Thaddeus warned.

"Shut the fuck up, Thad, or I'll add you to my goddamned list! You're my lawyer! This is confidential, private, so who the fuck cares what I say to you! Jesus you're such a whiny-ass shit sometimes! I don't know why I put up with you. These guys—they all go down, you hear me! And the goddamned Timofeyevs! They go down too. Those punk-ass pieces of shit started this and by God I'm going to end it. If Homeland Security wants someone to blame, it's them, not me. You tell them I'll testify against them! Tell them! We're in business together, but I don't need this shit!

Maybe I can do the deal with the other oligarchs. Christ what a mess.

"What do I care what the Russians are doing, for God's sake, as long as I make money? It's none of my business! But I tell you. Now? I'm not so sure anymore. Maybe I just need to pull out of those deals. Goddamn it, I'll lose a fortune! So that can't happen, Thad. Can you get me out of them on some moral's clause? Make up some bullshit if you need to. Because let me make this clear: I am not going to go down for this. The Timofeyevs can fry for it. I'll even light the goddamned match. Be sure to tell that fucking rat, Clarence, that he better back off this story and make them print a retraction that says I'm innocent, and I'll give them the Russians. They need a scapegoat. Fine. I'll burn my fucking deals, but you better mitigate the damage. We need to get on this. My reputation's on the line. In the goddamned *Post*! The hell do they think they're dealing with over there? I'm Hyde Sutton! Shut those papers down!"

He carried on for a while until Karla heard him bring up Owen: "You know, the other night I met this asshole from Homeland right before this went down, and he told me, *told* me they were going after the Timofeyevs, but I didn't say anything because I wanted to protect my investments. So, Homeland...they were looking at them before this, so this is on *them*, not on me. You should tell special agent Clarence to talk to Daniel Parks. Why don't they already know I'm innocent?"

"Do I need to remind you that I cautioned you against conducting business with the Timofeyev family? They have a reputation and ties to organized crime. We specifically discussed this, Hyde."

"But business is business! And besides, it was Roman, not his father. *Roman* has never been convicted of a crime in his life, right? So there's a difference here."

"It's the Timofeyev name, Hyde..."

And on it went. Karla sent the audio to Alex as soon as it was over to hear it for himself.

IN HIS OFFICE the next morning, Alex and Michael listened to the rant. Alex felt the warmth of adrenaline rush through him and made the decision. He flipped off the recorder on the old-fashioned Dictaphone he'd used to rerecord the call.

"We got him, Michael. It might not be enough, but it's the best we're going to get."

Alex picked up the Dictaphone and walked over to a big brown box on his desk. He wiped his prints off the small device and dropped it inside. The machine contained a "best ofs" clips of Hyde Sutton ranting to his lawyer, including, and especially, portions of the last duplicitous conversation.

He pointed to the box, counting the items inside: "Images of Daniel Parks, Homeland Security agent, wearing his jacket, looking concerned and busy at the Timofeyev warehouse the night of the raid. An image of Daniel Parks and his Homeland Security partner entering Sutton Tower, time stamped before the raid. A video of Daniel Parks in what appears to be a conspiratorial moment of him overflowing with gratitude while talking to Hyde in the lobby of his building on the night of the raid."

Alex turned and picked up a copy of the *New York Post* and dumped it on top. "Just in case they missed it."

He then plucked up the final item. Holding it by a corner, he laid the forged document on top. "A doctored copy of

Hyde Sutton's latest bank statement with a particular deposit highlighted."

Dated the day of the raid, $100,000 was supposedly deposited into Hyde's account from an unknown, offshore bank from a company only listed as RFJP. Next to it was handwritten, "Rewards for Justice Program."

Wadding up some newspaper, he threw it in the box, closed the lid, and stared at the addressee: Roman Timofeyev in Brooklyn.

He looked at his brother Michael, who hung his head. They were ready. It was done. But before they dropped the package in the mail, the phone rang. The call changed everything.

Chapter 34

"MARRIED?" ALEX SAID, his eyes narrowing in confusion. "What the...? You've got be kidding me. Owen and Carey got *married*?"

Charlotte laughed. "That's what I'm telling you! I just got a call from Mom, and she doesn't know what to think. Apparently, Carey and Owen Kai eloped—at a justice of the peace in Connecticut, of all places. They're hiding out in some cabin, apparently on their honeymoon."

"I don't believe this. They just met!" Alex sat back in a chair, his mouth hanging open.

"I know. And what about poor Harley? That's been going on forever, and I thought they were getting along really well at Charles's wedding. I guess not. When Mom asked her about him, she said they were just too different. He didn't approve of some of the things she did, and she didn't like it. I guess he was pressuring her to change."

Alex ran his hand through his hair. "Well what about Owen? Marrying someone is going to make her change, for crying out loud. She married him?"

"Also, no prenup, if you can believe it. She just did it. He must be really something to have convinced her to marry him so fast. I mean, we both saw the chemistry when they met, and we knew they were staying together at the Carlyle, but this is just crazy!"

"My God," Alex said, shaking his head. "Owen? He never seemed like the type of guy to settle down either. Why would they do this? What was the rush?"

Charlotte's voice was filled with enthusiasm. "She told Mom that they both just *knew*. It was love at first sight or something. I know, it's incredible. I guess Dad is having a fit over the prenup thing. He's already got poor Oliver trying to figure out a way to have Owen sign something after the fact. Do you think he'll do it?"

"I have no idea. I have no idea about anything anymore. This is nuts. And we've been using him on this latest business heavily. We were just getting ready to make a move here. A big one."

"Well, I think you should hold up on that, Alex. We need to reconsider everything now that he's a part of the family. I'll text you the wedding pictures she sent to Mom. They're pretty sweet. She had on a simple dress, well, simple for her, actually pretty modest, but super pretty, and he has on a nice suit. They looked like a couple of kids staring at each other with stars in their eyes. It's like two comets hitting. This is so great."

Alex rubbed his head. "Wow. Okay. I'll let Michael know. Jeez. Owen's our employee; you'd think he'd have the decency to let us know about something this monumental. He knows how far the Hyde project has gone and what we're doing. He's been in on it every step of the way."

"I doubt he's your employee any longer, Alex. He's your brother-in-law now."

Alex froze as Charlotte carried on: "She told Mom that they wanted to be alone for a couple of weeks, and then she wants to bring him out to California. I think if Mom and Dad have settled down by then, Mom's going to go into full party mode. The thing is, Angelica's staying with them, and the babies are due pretty soon, so yeah, it's a lot for them. Mom was talking about meeting Owen's family, and Carey told her they're in Hawaii."

"You don't think Carey's pregnant, do you?" Alex stared at the phone.

"She didn't say she was, and I don't think they've had quite enough time; well maybe they have. If she is, I still don't see it as a reason to get married. But it's done. Carey asked Mom, of all people, if *she* would call Harley so he won't hear about the marriage from anyone else. Can you believe it."

Alex snorted. "I can. What did Charles say?"

"He mostly wanted to know about *this guy*, this *Owen Kai*. He wants you to call him."

"Yeah, yeah, I'll call him right after I talk to Michael, because this changes everything."

"Yes it does. Forever. I hope they didn't make a mistake, Alex. She sure seems happy right now. I'm glad for that."

"I should have frickin' known I couldn't bring those two together. Impetuous, free-spirited, they were like a speeding train once they got together with neither one of them capable of putting on the brakes. Maybe it was a shag, marry, or kill thing? They had to mate and marry or they'd devour each other."

Charlotte laughed. "Stop. Let's call them together tonight. I know the business part is going to change now, but we need to support them as family, so let's congratulate them properly, and try to keep the scolding to a minimum."

"We have a lot invested on this, Charlotte. Time, money, plans, details."

"I get it. But now their happiness comes first. It's the most important thing."

"Wow. I gotta talk to Michael," he said.

"I wonder if she'll change her name?"

"To Carey Carrows Kai?" Alex squished up his face at the ridiculous sound of it.

"It's got a ring to it. Oh my God, they have matching gold bands! I never thought in a million years that she would do something like that. I thought she'd rob the Taj Mahal to get what she wanted in that department. Maybe she knew he couldn't afford anything bigger?"

"He probably just went out and bought the ring at a drugstore and slipped it on her finger. My God, I can see it all now."

"I think it's sweet. You know, as much trouble as we've had over the years, I've always hoped and wondered what would happen if Carey had someone in her life who would make her so deliriously happy that she wouldn't feel the need to be so snarky and mean. I wonder if Owen Kai will change her for the better."

"We're only spectators for this one, honey. God only knows."

Chapter 35

ALEX CALLED MICHAEL into his office and told him to close the door and take a seat. He broke the news.

"He did *what*? Now what are we going to do? And they didn't have a prenup?"

"Nope."

"That's incredible. With all the money she'll come into, Henry Carrows must be furious." Michael grimaced.

Alex ran a hand through his hair and blinked, still stunned. "I think he is. Julia and Angelica will calm him down though. It's a done deal, so we all have to accept it. Interesting that he hasn't called either one of *us* poor schmucks. I mean, he knows we're getting ready to send the package to the Timofeyevs and how hard we've worked to pull this off. It's how they met in the first place."

Michael shook his head. "I was only joking the other day when we talked about them shacking up at the Carlyle. I mean, I didn't really believe anything would happen. Not this, at any rate."

Looking at the brown box sitting on his desk, Alex continued, "Well it changes everything. Charlotte's right about that. We need to rethink the whole plan."

Michael looked a bit circumspect. "You know, Alex, I've got to say it's really interesting timing. If I'm honest with you, I've been feeling a bit apprehensive about the plan anyway."

"What are you talking about?" Alex frowned. "If you had reservations, you should have spoken up. I thought you were totally on board."

Michael shrugged. "I was. I still am. It's just that when a campaign starts and builds momentum, it's hard to stop and ask ourselves whether we're doing the right thing. I get that Hyde Sutton is a bad guy. I get that. But if we send the Timofeyevs that brown box, then we've made a huge leap into an area that I'm not all that sure I'm comfortable with."

Alex felt a headache coming on as he listened to his brother.

"If we send that box, then the Timofeyevs might kill him. You know that—and I know that. And based on what? They'll kill him because we're going to make them believe Hyde ratted them out, even though he didn't. Essentially, we did, and if they kill Hyde over what we send them, then we're responsible, and that bothers me."

"We don't *know* they'll kill him..." Alex looked at him under hooded brows.

Michael paused and returned the look with a hard, challenging one of his own. "You're right, Alex. We don't. I think we all *hoped* they'd just mess him up. Punish him. Let him know he can't get away with anything he wants and remind him of his responsibility over there in Bay Ridge."

"That's right, and he gave the keys to the Russian mob to use for smuggling humans. *Hyde* did that."

Michael put up a hand. "He did. You're right. And we did the right thing by shutting it down. That feels good, Alex. And what Charlotte's doing for the victims feels great. But now the authorities are investigating Hyde, and the legal process is in the works. If it works the way it's supposed to, then Hyde will get what's coming to him through those channels. If he doesn't, well, there's always tomorrow. In the meantime, we've tarnished his reputation, and he's in a world of trouble with Homeland Security. I think, and I've been thinking about this for a while, that it's enough. We're not the cops. We're not lawyers. Or at least not practicing lawyers anyway. Our job is security and private investigation, and we do that extremely well."

Alex shook his head, but Michael plowed on. "Hey, we uncovered a human trafficking ring, and we stopped it. That's a good thing. But the revenge business, I get it, and I'm not saying that we shouldn't nudge things sometimes, but this one? Alex, this is the Russian mafia. This is the Timofeyev family. Hyde Sutton was stupid enough to work with them, but if we send them the box, then *we're* working with them too."

Alex looked away and didn't respond. Michael used the opportunity to continue: "And now, there's Owen and Carey. The Carrows are too high profile. Carey Carrows getting married, there will be press, and Owen's face is going to be out there. *Owen Kai.* Our guy. Our coolest undercover guy, he's going to be in the press, forever connected to you. To the Carrows. To the Macchis. Are we really going to send the head of the Russian mafia pictures of *your brother-in-law*, pretending to be an agent at Homeland Security? Pretending to be in cahoots with Hyde Sutton to bring about their destruction?"

Alex put his head down and mumbled, "Fuck."

"They'll have his picture, Alex. It's not going to work. Roman has met Owen in person and seen him with Carey. What if Roman finds out the whole government-job thing was a ruse? What then? Look, we can't take back that meeting at the Sloan Kettering Ball, but let's not throw a spotlight on it for them and tie Owen to Hyde. I'm glad this happened, Alex. Because now we have to stop. We *can't* send that box. We need to protect your brother- and sister-in-law from any more exposure. The Timofeyevs? Forget *them*, Alex. *Henry Carrows* would kill us both if anything happened to his daughter."

Alex pulled his head up and looked to Michael's earnest face. He wasn't happy, but he was listening.

"Macchi & Macchi wasn't designed for this, Alex; it's just too big. Owen is no longer an employee who could just disappear into the woodwork, back on his board in Hawaii, where neither Hyde nor the Timofeyev's would have ever found him. He married a Carrows, and like it or not, he'll now be a public figure."

Alex knew Michael was right, but it was still hard to hear. He stared at the box. The job was so personal for him. Somewhere along the way, he'd recognized that his plan might have big consequences, but he'd felt it was the right thing to do. Hyde Sutton needed to be stopped, whatever the cost. At least that's what he'd told himself.

"Michael, I didn't know you felt like that and I wish you'd spoken up earlier. If I'm honest with myself, I've had a moment or two when I wondered if I was doing the right thing. Charlotte's questioned me too. We're partners and brothers, though, and I figured that if you weren't stopping me, you thought what we were doing was right."

Michael shrugged.

Alex lowered his voice. "I didn't tell Charlotte what I did to Hyde's bank statement, and that should've given me pause. When I start hiding things from Charlotte, it might be because I know she's not going to approve."

His brother smirked at him. Alex inhaled deeply. "So all right then. We stop now, with one exception. I think we should keep listening in to Hyde while this thing is hot. I want to be forewarned and ready to protect ourselves if something wicked this way comes."

Michael put his head back in relief then let out a deep breath. "I agree. And, Alex, you're not a bad guy to have as a partner. I'm proud of you. But next time, I'll let you know when I think you're going too far." He stood and slowly edged toward the brown package, as if it were ready to explode, and picked it up. "Now I'm going to take this ticking time bomb and lock it away before it falls into the wrong hands. We'll let the Feds sort out Hyde, and we'll sort out Owen Kai. Do you want to fire him or should I?" Michael smiled as he walked to the door with the box.

Alex bit his lip staring at the departing box and realized that he, too, was relieved they were retreating—sort of. "Well since he's family now, I don't want to fire him, you do it. I've got to go home to a giddy wife and make a happy call welcoming him to the family."

Michael smirked. "You know, he's got to be a little worried about what's happening over here and if his face is being sent to the Timofeyevs. He knew the plan. You'd think he would have called us to give us a heads-up. Why are we the only ones who are worried about him and the family?"

"I don't think he's really thinking about anything right now, Michael. Owen Kai has left the building."

Chapter 36

THAT EVENING ALEX stood near his wife as she called Carey and Owen to congratulate them. Carey was wild with excitement, and it was contagious. Charlotte practically danced as she joined in the fun. "I'm so happy for you, Carey! You sound wonderful. Mom and Dad will relax once they meet Owen, I'm sure. He has a way about him!"

Alex rolled his eyes at Charlotte.

"He surely does," said Carey.

"Yes, uh, ladies," said Owen, sounding nervous. "Charlotte, Alex, thank you for your blessing. It means a great deal to us both. We would have invited you to the wedding, but it just felt right for us to be alone. What we had to say was very private, very personal, and we didn't want an audience."

"We had witnesses, of course," said Carey. "The justice of the peace and his wife, but that was it. It was so intimate. So real. It was the most amazing moment of my life. I'm so lucky that I found him."

"And I'm lucky that I found you, Carey. My beautiful blushing bride."

Alex shook his head and mouthed *Oh my God* as Charlotte beamed. They listened to the newlyweds, sickeningly coo and share stories about the wedding and their newfound love. The ridiculousness of the situation was easier to swallow because his wife's happiness also bloomed.

"Well when can we see you and celebrate?" Charlotte gushed.

"Soon, I hope, but we've got to get to California. Daddy's wild to meet him, and Mom's already demanding we have some kind of formal reception out there."

Charlotte said, "Charles is out there now. They've only got a week or so until the babies. Why don't you let Mom plan something, Carey? You know it would make her feel better. Maybe you can go out next week before the babies so they can meet Owen, and then, after the babies are born and Angelica's on her feet, Mom and Dad could throw a big reception and Owen's family could come over. After a short visit to Whispering Cliffs, maybe you could go to Hawaii to meet his family and then all come back for the party? You could honeymoon some more on the islands while you're waiting."

"That's an excellent idea, Charlotte," Owen said, being very agreeable.

Alex rolled his eyes again as Owen rambled on. "We were thinking something like that would work for us. My parents are very anxious to meet Carey too as you can imagine."

"Tell me about your family, Owen. Do you have brothers and sisters? Which island does your family live on?" Charlotte asked.

"I've got a couple of brothers, but they're quite a bit older than me. I was what you call a love child, born a little late in the marriage, so my brothers and I are really far apart in age. Mom and Dad live on Maui, and that's where I usually stay. Dad's a planter, or rather he is one now. He worked for IBM for years but then bought a small coffee bean farm and they have sort of settled into that lifestyle. My brothers and their families live on the Big Island."

"I can't wait to meet them!" squealed Carey.

Owen laughed, "My brothers are going to love you. My parents too. I know it. They're awfully surprised, but they were really happy for us. I'm the last bird in their nest, so I think they're glad to see me settled."

"So let's get over there," said Carey, happily piping in. "Let's catch a plane to California tomorrow and meet my parents and Charles and Angelica before the place goes into baby overdrive, then we'll hop over to meet your family."

"That sounds perfect, honey," said Owen dripping with sweetness at her every utterance.

Alex grabbed the phone, holding it close to his mouth like a walkie-talkie. "Oh hey," he said, "don't worry about your job or anything over here, okay. Owen? We've got it covered, but give Michael a call when you have a minute; he needs to talk to you about something."

Carey said, "Don't scold him, Alex. He couldn't help himself. Really, it was like magic for both of us. You just have no idea what this feels like. It's like we live on another planet and we're the only ones on it. It's the most amazing feeling in the world."

Alex put down the phone and walked away, staring at the ceiling. Charlotte laughed, "We'll meet you in California then at the reception. Have a wonderful visit with Mom and Dad and Charles and Angelica, and give them a kiss from all of us. Welcome to the family, Owen Kai. We couldn't be happier for you both."

After they hung up, Charlotte jumped and ran into his arms. "I've never in my *life* heard her so happy. If Owen makes her feel like this, then what a *gift* he is to all of us. I've always wished I had a sister who I could feel close to. Maybe finding happiness with Owen will make that happen."

Alex smiled at his sentimental wife and kissed her, "It's wonderful, honey, and if they have even a little of what we do, then they're very lucky. You never know what life has in store for you. I'm glad they found each other."

Chapter 37

Freya Brown sat on the beach looking out to the ocean, thinking about what her life meant to her. She shielded her eyes as she looked down the long strip of white sand and at a seagull pecking his way toward her. The ocean waves crashed against the shore and she turned to look at the sea. *What a big world it is*, she thought. *I've crossed oceans and swam through hell to get to this stretch of beach.*

She pulled her knees up to her chest and folded her head in her lap and cried. Hot raking sobs that she couldn't control. She was desperately tired of the tears, but she couldn't stop, and it scared her. She missed her family and she wanted to retreat to the world of her childhood where everything was safe, and she was loved. She tried hard to remind herself that she was still loved, very much, but it wasn't the same anymore. She had changed. Being abducted would do that to you.

The constant fear she'd faced while she was in captivity, the waking realization that she was lost to her family and her world, that no one would ever be able to find her, and that her destiny and life were violently ripped away from her had been her constant thoughts. It was almost too much to process, but after the days of captivity became weeks, she realized that she was living in a nightmare and she would never wake up. The only thing that gave her comfort, some hope at all, was that she wasn't alone. Surrounded by other women who were living in the same hellish dream, she could reach out and touch them and be reminded that she and they were still real, still people, women, and human beings.

The experience would be burned into her heart and her mind, and especially her soul, for the rest of her life. And that was troubling her greatly. Because as she was coming back into her previous life, she could feel the damaged part of her soul wanting to break free. Her traumatized mind was telling her that it was over, that she was safe, but her heart had yet to catch up and it frightened her because she didn't know if it ever would.

She was also experiencing terrible guilt. Survivor's guilt her counselor called it, because she'd been one of the lucky few that had not been raped. She'd watched in horror as most of the other women on the boat, on the long journey with endless transfers, were raped and beaten in front of her. She didn't know why she had escaped that personal horror.

The other women didn't want to see her raped, but they also knew that she and another young woman named Tina were the only two who had been spared this torture. But she'd been humiliated in other ways. Violated and groped by the men demanding her to strip, they touched her naked body on a number of occasions and rubbed themselves against her. Several times they demanded all of them strip at the same time, none of them knowing which one in the pack would be next. The cumulative effect of everything that had happened had turned her into someone she didn't know.

Her teeth chattered with the memories and her body shook as another wave took hold of her. She cried some more. It was who she'd become.

Chapter 38

CHARLOTTE ENTERED THE BEACH HOUSE for the first time since the women had arrived. Speaking privately with Sarah, the two women walked outside to the porch. Sarah pointed to the beach and to Freya, who was sitting under an umbrella alone.

Charlotte walked through the white sand toward the ocean and approached her. "Hello, I'm so sorry to disturb you, I was wondering if I could speak with you for a minute?"

Freya, appearing embarrassed by tears, dried her face on her shirt and put on her sunglasses and said, "No, it's okay."

Charlotte sat down in the sand a short distance from her, and said, "My name is Charlotte. Sarah has kept me posted, letting me know how things were going here, and I told her to call me if she thought of anything we could do for you and the other women, and I wanted to say hello."

"Are you a social worker too?"

Charlotte put her head down and played with the sand. Freya looked like a little kid, not all that much different than Petunia with her dark, curly hair. She swallowed hard and tried to keep the emotion out of her voice. "No. I work with an organization that helps people. I'd heard about the shortage of residential placement centers for victims of trafficking, so we bought this house to help with that shortage and give those rescued a nice safe place to stay. I mean, I don't know if it helps, really, but I thought just in case, I wanted to remind the survivors that there are people in the world who care, and there still is beauty in the world. I can't imagine what you've been through, but I thought, you know, it might help."

"*You* own this house?"

"I do, and I'm sorry about what's happened to you, Freya, and for what they did to all of the women. I don't really know what to say, because I feel like whatever I say, it won't be enough. I'm just so sorry."

Freya nodded her head in acceptance. "They've been telling us that we're survivors, you know, like we made it! Yay!" She hung her head before she continued, "I know they mean well. I get it. And I did survive, so yeah, it fits."

"I'm glad you're here, Freya, and many, many people all around the world would be cheering for you, glad you got out, and hoping for your recovery. But I know it's going to take time. Lots of time, but Sarah tells me she thinks you're a fighter, and that's good. The experts, they tell me it should help." Charlotte hung her head and spoke more softly, "She also told me that you miss your parents and that it's frustrating because the process is taking so long. She said that you told her you were worried they couldn't afford to come over, and that your dad's a carpenter? Is that right?"

The young girl nodded and looked away.

"Freya, I hope you don't mind, but I called them."

Charlotte felt surprise and fear as Freya turned on her with anger. "Why'd you do that? Now they'll feel guilty because they don't have the money to travel to New York City, America, and rent a car, and stay in hotels. They've been through enough!"

"I don't think you understand. I didn't call them to make them feel guilty. I called them and told them there were airplane tickets waiting for them at the Edinburgh airport for a direct flight to New York. I paid for them Freya, so no worries, I have more than enough to go around. Your mom and dad are on their way here right now, honey. They landed in New York almost three hours ago, and I had a driver pick them up at the airport. They'll be here very shortly."

Charlotte watched in horror as the poor girl released a terrible moan, and her entire body began to tremble. Tears ran down her face and Charlotte, in such close proximity, couldn't help herself. She reached over and held her.

"It's okay, Freya, it's okay," she said as she comforted her. "I asked Sarah to bring them down here to the beach when they arrived, so you could have a private reunion away from the other women. We'll do what we can for their families, too, so don't worry about that. It was you who gave us the idea. So you know, I've paid for a room for your parents at a bed and breakfast, a small hotel, in town, just down the way, since there's no room here in the house. You can stay with them there, if you'd like, while they visit."

Freya trembled in her arms and couldn't stop sobbing. The front of Charlotte's shirt was soaked with the young girl's tears as she saw from the corner of her eyes, Sarah, coming out of the house with two older people. As they started walking toward them, Charlotte released her and said softly, "Freya, angel, they're here."

Charlotte watched as the young girl pulled up sharply, wiped her face on her shirt, and ran across the beach toward her parents who were running toward her.

It's a start, Charlotte breathed, *a good start.*

Chapter 39

An associate district attorney by the name of Virgil Reese and several other representatives of law enforcement agencies had gathered the women of the house and their interpreters to talk about the legal case against their abductors. Freya Brown and her parents were also there to listen.

"The night of the raid, we arrested over thirty individuals we believed were either directly involved in the human-trafficking ring or were customers. There will most likely be others arrested, all along the chain, but for now, to keep things manageable for this discussion, I'd like to focus on the events that took place once you entered the United States. The ten of you staying in this house represent a contained group we have been referring to as 'the Eclipse Ten,' which is a reference to the name of the boat, the 'Eclipse,' that delivered you to this country. There were a number of other women who were victims of this particular ring, but they had been on U.S. soil longer, and their circumstances are different. Your circumstances were roughly similar. I understand that you each were abducted from a variety of cities and that the crimes that have been committed against you are not exactly the same, but for our purposes here today, we have you organized into this group.

"During your time together, you witnessed the criminals who were a part of the ring—specifically, the two men arrested on the Eclipse, and the four men from the vans who were also apprehended at the scene. It's my job to prosecute those six particular men. Other attorneys will be prosecuting the rest of the criminals, and there'll be some overlap of charges, but that does not concern us today for this discussion.

"From the statements you've already given, those six were the only men you encountered while on U.S. soil, which is why we are focusing on them right now. As the Eclipse Ten, you are potential eyewitnesses for the prosecution and could be called to testify against them in court. What I need today is an understanding about your willingness to participate in a U.S. trial, or your reluctance to do so and the reasons why. You should know that if you choose to testify, it will be easier for all of us if you stayed here in country until this portion of the trials have been completed. Temporary visas, which are already being gathered for you, will be extended should you testify.

"I know you've been reading about the people who may have been involved in the papers, so you've probably gathered that we believe the ring has its roots in the Russian mafia. There are ties in St. Petersburg, where several of you are from, and locally in the United States. We are working with the U.S. and Russian governments to secure more arrests, but as I said, we're focusing on the six men arrested from the Eclipse and the vans. Eyewitness testimony will be crucial during the prosecution, but I won't lie to you: it will be stressful, painful, frustrating, and possibly dangerous. The Russian mafia, both in Russia and here in the States, is a dangerous criminal enterprise, and those involved may possibly take measures to protect their own. I'm not trying to discourage you from testifying, I'm just trying to be honest. Due to the potential dangers of testifying, the U.S. government—specifically the FBI—will protect you before, during, and after the trial in our witness protection program."

Virgil Reese gestured toward a woman standing near him. "This is FBI agent Tana Kipp. We don't want to cause any alarm, but we're installing her in the house, beginning today, for your protection."

There were a lot of nervous looks among the women, but Virgil plowed on: "In addition to the six men, you may be asked to participate in other trials for more charged individuals, but we won't be addressing that today. Suffice it to say that if you choose to help us and become part of the U.S. Witness Protection Program, then we'd appreciate your participation in as many of the trials that are pertinent. The T visas, which are temporary visas, will be given to those who are willing to stay and testify.

"Those who choose not to testify will be given your new identification materials and deported, and returned to your country within the next month. I would like to open this conversation up to questions, but before I do, can I see a show of hands who, at this stage, are interested in helping us bring these criminals to justice."

After the translators finished, the room was fearfully quiet as the women looked at one another to see who would raise their hands. No one did.

It was a difficult start, but the attorneys and FBI representative answered their questions about witness protection and what that would mean. The women had already sacrificed so much, they were understandably reluctant to give anymore and radically change what chance was left for them to resume their previous lives. But they might come around. At least that's what Virgil Reese hoped. If not, well, the government could still prosecute; it would just be better to put a face or two before the jury to make the crimes come alive.

But the women were, understandably, frightened, and the prosecutors were willing to give them some time to consider their options—but not too long.

Chapter 40

HYDE SUTTON WAS FEELING the heat, and he was pissed. Yelling at his lawyers had accomplished shit, and per usual, he had to fix everything. The way he saw it, he had four problems: He needed to turn around the bad publicity that was tarnishing his name; he needed to threaten the media so they would be too fearful to ever come after him again unless they had actual fucking pictures of him screwing some useless, teenaged Russian whore; he needed to make sure his team of overpaid, asshole lawyers kept the corrupt DA from filing *any* charges against him; and he needed to settle his business plans going forward with the Timofeyevs and the oligarchs.

He'd taken care of the ungrateful district attorney, whom he'd supported in the last election, by firing stupid Thad from the criminal investigation and hiring pit bulls who knew their way around criminal law and the political systems. If that jackass DA wanted to be reelected next year, he'd better slowly walk away from any bogus bullshit they were trying to pin on him and Mercer.

He kept stupid Thad and his team of henchmen on the media outlets, threatening litigation and beginning the process for the first round of salvos against the dumbass *Post* editors who ran the story after the raid. Since then, they'd been quiet, but of course, once the articles broke, the other news outlets reported on it. So he hired yet another team of public relation specialists who were out in the front of the story now and doing a hell of a job spit shining his beautiful, preexisting image.

The last piece was the money already on the table with Roman Timofeyev. The St. Petersburg and Prague deals were now on shaky ground, and that wasn't okay. None of the players had called him. Not Roman or his thug father, who was probably behind all this bullshit, or the other oligarchs. Hyde imagined the oligarchs didn't care about the publicity as much as he did since the publicity and story weakened as it traveled. But they still probably cared a little...or maybe a lot. What the hell did he know about how those Communist assholes felt about each other? Maybe they were also pissed at the Timofeyevs. It was a thought, but he needed to move carefully.

None of this was his fault. That was for damn sure. Roman and his father were to blame. What to do, what to do, what to do? He wasn't frightened of them, but he wanted to fix the problems and come out ahead. He'd already invested millions and wasn't about to walk away from it.

He'd instructed the idiot, Thad, to create another new company, one solely for the two Timofeyev deals. He would transfer all paperwork, all agreements, and all money to the new company and hide it from the rest of his businesses that had more transparency and exposure. That done, he could tell the world that he had severed ties from the Timofeyevs; but secretly, he'd still proceed. He wanted the profits, and it was leverage time.

He assumed the Timofeyevs were also moving ahead with the deals, but Hyde had not wanted to be the one to reach out. They were poison. But now that he'd secured clamps to halt the other bleeding, he got a burner phone and decided it was time to get in touch with the assholes.

ROMAN HAD BEEN on pins and needles, waiting for instructions from his father about next steps on every part of his life. Sitting in his Brooklyn kitchen, he didn't recognize the number on his cellphone but answered the call, "Hello."

"Roman. It's me. We've got to talk."

Roman stood up. He recognized the barking sound in Hyde's voice, but wasn't going to play lapdog. "Yes. How about you come to me, to my home, and we can speak here?"

"To your home, are you nuts? I'm sure the press would just love that!" Hyde spat.

Roman gritted his teeth and put his free hand in a claw, trying to be patient. "I need to speak with you in a safe place, and there's a room in my home that blocks all electronic eavesdropping or recordings. You could make it happen. Just don't use your regular driver or car service. Walk out the building and get into a cab. Wear something to blend in and change cabs a couple of times."

"What is this, some kind of spy movie? Why the hell would I go to all that trouble? How about you meet *me* on the street, *you wear something bland* that will *blend in*. I'll pull up, and you can hop in my car. We can talk in private while we drive around the city."

Roman squeezed his eyes shut and felt like he had a bad taste in his mouth. "How do I know it would be safe to talk in your car?"

"The fuck is this, Roman? You think I'm dumb enough to record it or something? Because I'm no chump, asshole. I'm Hyde Sutton, not some piece of shit off the bottom of your shoe from Brooklyn or Brighton Beach."

Roman couldn't believe the shit he had to take from this dick but decided it would be best to meet. Spreading the fingers on his free hand, he snarled, "Fine then. When and where?"

Chapter 41

TWO DAYS LATER, a heated Roman sat in the back seat of Hyde Sutton's limousine as promised. Viktor had authorized the visit, but gave him a cellular-blocking signal to carry with him. Roman didn't feel completely secure, but agreed that he and Hyde needed to start somewhere.

"Roman, Roman," Hyde shook his head. "What am I going to do with you?"

He gave Hyde a level stare and sucked in his cheeks to suppress his anger as he endured the typical smugness on the man's face. "What do you mean? We need to talk about the business."

Hyde held a crystal tumbler and twirled the liquid while he spoke. "Yeah, we do, so let me tell you what's going to happen. You know and I know that our deals in St. Petersburg and Prague are too far along to stop. I've got way too much money tied up in them, and I've decided...not to back away because that's how much I believe in them. What I *could* do, however, is ask you to refund everything.

Everything I've put into it, but I've given it some thought, and think what we need to do is renegotiate."

Hyde overenunciated "re-ne-go-ti-ate," his lips pursed like a grotesque cartoon character. Roman wanted to punch his lights out.

"I think my percentage investment from this point forward goes down, and my percentage of the profits goes up. Out of *your* end, Roman. Consider it a penalty for all the bullshit you've caused me. My lawyers got everything drawn up, ready to go under a different corporation, taking my name—my *well-respected* name—out of it. I've got to protect myself from now on, and at least until this thing blows over, I don't want to be seen with you in public."

Hyde wobbled his head in triumph and made an idiotic smirk to punctuate the end of his lecture before taking a huge sip of what Roman knew was a girly, bubbly, diet soda.

Stay calm. Roman worked to control his temper. "I need to give it some thought, Hyde."

"Well, how about this? If you don't give me everything I want, you leave your investment in and drop out entirely. Then *I'll* renegotiate with the oligarch crowd, and you can go back to Brooklyn to do God knows what with your *dad-dy.*"

"Stop the car. I've heard enough."

Hyde smiled like he knew he had won. "Sure, sure," he said, pushing a button for the screen to come down slightly. He yelled for the driver to pull over.

Roman grabbed the handle of the door and as he got out, he heard Hyde say: "Get back to me on that last number. Got it?"

Roman slammed the door and walked down the street. He felt fucking sick about having to report this to his father. He walked the streets, considering his options, and eventually landed in a small park, where he screwed up the courage to call his father.

The report exchanged, Viktor said, "Bring him in, Roman. It's time I let him know time of day. I want him in room."

Roman closed his eyes. "Okay. I'll see what I can do to get him there."

STILL THREE FLOORS BELOW Hyde Sutton, Karla Fernandez watched the lion pace. By now, she recognized he was at a boiling point, which meant he was about to unload on someone. He'd just taken a call on his burner phone, apparently from Roman Timofeyev, and they'd argued about meeting at Roman's house. Hyde was furious that he was being told what to do, but said he just wanted to get it over with. "Fine. I'll come to you. Do you see how reasonable I can be? After all this shit, *I'm* the one being reasonable. Next Tuesday night I've got some time; I'll be by at nine. Is that *okay* with you, Roman?"

Hyde had capitulated and agreed to the meet, but now he was furious and muttering, "Goddamned Timofeyevs. I gotta straighten them out. Like goddamned children, everyone needs to be told what to do all the time, and I'm the only one with the answers. Shit!"

For the first time, Karla watched Hyde do something unprecedented. He walked to a bookcase and revealed a safe that she hadn't known existed. He entered a code, opened the door, and rifled through a number of items, including papers, cash, and finally, a handgun. He held it in his hand and opened it to check the ammunition and mumbled what Karla later reported she thought was: "If I'm going over there, I'm going heavy."

Having leaned closely to her monitor to watch the action, she pulled her face back. "Whoa. What an incredible jackass."

Hyde put the gun back in the safe and closed the door. Angrily, he stomped across the room. threw open his office door, and screamed, "Pravdina! Prav! Get in here!"

Karla groaned and realized the poor woman was in for another long night.

Chapter 42

HYDE SUTTON SUPPOSED he was no Jason Bourne, but heading out several nights later for his Tuesday assignation in Brooklyn, he thought he looked the part. He did what Roman suggested and wore casual black pants and a black T-shirt. He also carried his small-caliber handgun in his light black overcoat. Going out the front of his building, he walked down the street and hailed a taxi.

Realizing he didn't have a conceal and carry permit, he figured the odds of him being caught by law enforcement that night were zero. Several blocks later, he got out at a department store, went inside, exited from a different door, and hailed another taxi. This went on for some time until he finally remained in one that dropped him a block from Roman's house in Brooklyn. Walking up to the door, he had to admit it was somewhat exhilarating to play the game, but now he just wanted the meeting over.

Roman opened the door and let him in. "Thanks for coming. Let's talk in the other room." Roman led him to the basement, but before entering through another closed door, he said, "You need to leave your phone on the table here before we go inside, so I know you're not recording anything."

"This is bullshit, Roman, and you know it," said Hyde as he, nevertheless, complied. "What about you? Where's your fucking phone?"

Roman took it out of his pocket, laid it next to Hyde's, and gestured toward the door. "Shall we?"

"Sure," Hyde said, making a face.

Entering the room, Hyde blinked, surprised to see Viktor. Trying to remain unaffected, he said, "Viktor, didn't know you'd be joining us." He shot Roman a disgusted look.

"Have seat, Mr. Sutton. I wish speak to you," said Viktor.

"Sure. Sure. I wish speak to you too, so let's get this started. Let me begin." Hyde pulled out a wooden chair and sat. "The two of you are pretty close, huh?" he said, wagging his finger between them. "So Roman told you about my offer? I'll stay in the partnership, but you gotta make it worth my while now that you two have fucked it up royally and made my life difficult.

"Do you have *any* idea how much money I've spent in legal fees? It's unbelievable! And the press? What about them? The goddamned press had to be dealt with. I've had to hire some hot-shot PR place to deal with the blowout. I've got attorneys, *criminal attorneys*, now working for me, and costing me a goddamned fortune. Never, never had to deal with this kind of bullshit before. Frankly, I think I should send all the bills your way. This deal is costing me money, real money, my money, and I told Roman that we need to restructure this thing so I can come out ahead. Otherwise, this is just bullshit what I've had to go through, and I'll do something else. I'm telling you, and I gave

Roman here a heads-up, because I'm that kind of guy, you have an opportunity to get this right with me. One last chance. Once last opportunity tonight, or I'm going to go to the oligarchs and deal with them directly. You choose, because frankly, I think I'm being very generous, given the fact that I've had to deal with so much shit. That you caused. On *my* property," he said, pointing his shooter fingers at both Roman and Viktor.

"Consider it a penalty fee, Viktor, but I've got something coming my way on this, and you know it. So why don't you tell me about the plan that you two have cooked up and give me several *million* reasons why I should stay in business with you?"

Viktor spread his legs wide and crossed his arms across his chest. "Yes, penalty fee. Roman told me about this plan. But first, I ask you questions."

Hyde threw out his hand in a magnanimous gesture to proceed, but pulled his head back when Viktor leaned toward him like an animal, growling. "Did you go to cops? Do you work for police?"

Hyde's mouth dropped open. "What? What the fuck are you talking about? Of course I had to talk to them after the raid in Bay Ridge. They brought in everyone from Mercer. I just told you I had to hire *criminal* attorneys to deal with this!"

"This is not what I mean. I mean, did you go to cops *before* raid?"

Hyde returned Viktor's menacing stare. "What the hell are you talking about? Of course I didn't fucking talk to the cops about anything. Why would I do that?" He paused and glared into the angry prick's eyes, challenging him to shut his shit down. Looking over to Roman, he side-nodded for support, but there too, only got a hostile look back. Hyde turned back to Viktor and said, "I don't know what the hell you're implying here, but I never spoke with the cops. Never."

"What about man from Homeland Security you met at Sloan Kettering Ball?"

Hyde felt a small lump in his throat, realizing they were talking about Daniel Parks. He had no idea how they knew about him. "What man?"

Roman said, "I saw you speaking with a Homeland Security guy the night of the ball. When I asked you about it, you lied and told me you were working a real estate deal with him."

Startled that they knew who he was, he nevertheless shrugged. "Hey, it's no big deal. We were just talking. I didn't want to spook you or anything, and besides, it's my business who I talk to, but I can promise you that I *wasn't* talking to them about you."

"Them?" asked Viktor.

Hyde opened his mouth in annoyance and shook his head. "The agency. Anyone. The cops. I didn't tell them anything. Why would I do that?"

"To take us out of equation," Viktor sneered at him.

"No. Now look! I had nothing to do with any of this. You're the ones who made a mess out of this, and I blame you! I mean, let's be honest here, I knew you had a repute-tion. I knew the name *Timofeyev.* Everyone knows it. Do you think I'm stupid? But I didn't let that stand in my way because business is business, and I was willing to do a deal with Roman *Timofeyev* here, to give you a chance to work with some *legitimate* businesspeople at the big table. I *gave* you that chance. I figured that whatever else you have going, you'd have the brains to keep it away from our deals. Because my deals always make money. Always.

"And you had a legitimate business development that I was willing to invest in because it was a winner. You know it, I know it, and that's the only reason I ever do business with anybody. Why the hell would I risk my good name and bring all this shit down on my head? Because I'm a patriot? A good guy? I'm a businessman, and I make money. That's it! So stuff those accusations back in the box of paranoia that you have when you work with other people, because I'm a straight-up guy. I thought we had a legitimate chance to make some money together. I wouldn't fuck it up. *You* did that! You did that on one of my properties, and now the whole world can be reminded what the Timofeyev name is all about."

Hyde pointed his finger in Viktor's face. "I gave you a tremendous opportunity to finally be legitimate and *this* is how you thank me? By accusing me of ratting you out? I didn't have a fucking clue what you were doing over there, so I couldn't talk to anyone about shit. But now look at me? *I'm* paying for it in the press! I'm going to sue those bastards, and I'm going to win because I didn't know shit, and I didn't talk to anyone. About anything. So you take your accusations back. I'm a businessman, and this is bullshit."

Viktor seemed to listen patiently while the steam poured out of Hyde. He said, "Okay, Mr. Sutton. I'm going to make something crystal clear to you. In case you don't understand who you are dealing with, I have reputation too. I am businessman too. I always get what I want, and no one ever screws me over and gets away with it. I don't know if you rat on us to police. I don't know…but," he reached into his jacket pocket, pulled out two pictures, and put them face-down on the table. "I have two cards that I will play if I find out you have betrayed us. This is deadly serious game. I am deadly serious man. You play your hand in business game, and I play mine."

One at a time, Viktor turned over pictures of Simone and Pravdina. "And you forfeit your family."

Hyde's eyes bulged from his face, and his heart hammered as he screamed at the madman, "What are doing? What is *wrong* with you? You can't threaten me. I'm Hyde Sutton! This is bullshit! If anything happens to me or my family, the cops will know exactly where to look! I'll make sure of it! I've already covered this with my lawyer, and they have documents that spell out *everything* should anything happen to me. Do you think I'm stupid? I took out an insurance plan and hoped I wouldn't have to use it, but now you're threatening my *family?* Are you nuts? You think the cops won't come after you? You can't touch me, asshole! You can't touch me!" he screamed.

The Arm pulled back and punched him in the face. Hyde's head bounced back, and he heard a loud crack as stars burst in his eyes. Pain, instant and intense, shot through his face and into his skull. His hands flew to his broken nose as blood began to pour down his face.

Roman yelled, "Dad, no!"

Viktor stood with his massive fists clenched and appeared ready to take another swing.

"Motherfucker!" Hyde yelled and stood. He put his hand in his pocket and pulled out his gun. He wobbled it in front of Viktor's face and watched Roman take a step back. "You broke my nose! You broke my nose! You'll pay for that! You hit me! God you hit me! You're not going to get away with it. I'm leaving here and going straight to the cops now. I'll have you arrested for assault. You assaulted me!"

With snot and blood making it hard to breathe, Hyde reached up to wipe away the fluids as Viktor's arm shot out and grabbed his wrist. Hyde screamed as the Russian pushed him against the wall and, with another sickening crunch, he heard his wrist break. He dropped the gun, wailing from the unimaginable pain, and fell to the floor.

Viktor kicked his prone body, while screaming, "You're dead! You're dead! You hear me! You're dead!"

Roman could hear the sound of his heart pounding as he scrambled to pick up Hyde's gun. The meeting had turned into a shit show. Grabbing his father by the arms, he somehow managed to pull him off Hyde and wrestle him out of the room. Locking it behind him, he tried to get control of the situation as his father continued screaming, "He's dead!"

"Dad! Calm down, keep your voice down! Settle down. It's okay. We got this." He watched his father pace menacingly back and forth as his own adrenaline coursed through his body.

Running his hand down his face, still holding Hyde's gun, Roman was shocked that things had gone so awry. He walked over to a bureau and put the gun in a drawer. Coming back to his panting father, he said, "Dad, you've got to calm down. I'm sorry, but we need to think now and decide what to do, and I *don't* want to do this in my hallway. Listen, I have an idea, so let's go back in there and discuss it with him. Can you hear me? I've got this. Okay," he said, looking for some reassurance that his father understood.

Viktor pushed past him and went into the room where Hyde was still on the floor, holding his wrist and whimpering about needing a doctor.

Roman closed the door and said loudly, "We're going to get him out to the car and take him to the hospital. Dad, we have to. He needs medical attention, and you've done enough. He's not going to hurt us; he's not going to tell the cops how this happened, he's going to tell them he was mugged. Isn't that right, Hyde?" Roman yelled the last sentence at Hyde.

His father paced around Hyde's curled and wounded body like a hungry tiger looking at live prey suddenly tossed in his cage. Roman screamed at Hyde. "You were mugged. Say it."

"Yes, I was mugged. I won't tell anyone. I won't. Just get me to the hospital. God, I can see a bone sticking out; I'm going to be sick."

Roman turned to his father, his eyes wide, and pleaded with him. "See, Dad. He's promised. He's going to tell them he was mugged. Because, Hyde, are you listening? You cannot tell anyone anything else, because if you do, my dad will find you. He'll find you and your family. You know that, right? He's not someone to let that go. Again. You pulled *a gun* on us, Hyde. *You* did that, so this is *your* fault. He'll kill you all, Hyde. You and your family. Do you hear me? Nod if you hear me."

Hyde nodded and started blubbering.

Roman ran a hand across his mouth as his father continued pacing, as if waiting to be fed. Viktor was capable of ripping a man's arm out of its' socket. Among other effective torture and bloodletting techniques, he'd seen the breadth of his father's violence firsthand. Hyde had it coming, but Roman couldn't let it happen. "All right then, both of you. All is well. Now let's get him in the car. I'll get some towels down in the back seat and we'll drive him to the hospital. This has gone far enough. Is everyone calm now?" he said loudly to them both, "Can I trust the two of you to remain calm and let this be over? Hyde, do we have your word here? I'm trying to help you."

"Yes, you have my word," he cried.

"Dad, do I have your word that you won't hurt him again, and we can get him some medical attention?"

Roman tried not to grimace but felt his stomach lurch waiting for a blow to even land on him, but was gratified when Viktor looked at him with some sense in his eyes. "Trust me," he beseeched his father through clenched teeth.

"Yes, okay." Viktor relented.

Roman nodded. "All right then. Hyde! We're going to step out of the room and get some towels, and then we're going to take you to the hospital. Dad, come with me."

After he shut the door on the room, Roman whispered in his father's ear, "After we get him in the car, you knock him unconscious; I have an idea."

Viktor inhaled and placed a hard hand on Roman's shoulder. He gave him a half smile and seemed much happier with the new plan. After that, he followed the instructions to a tee.

With Hyde Sutton unconscious in the back seat next to his father, Roman pulled out into the night and slowly drove south from Brooklyn into Bay Ridge. When they neared the old complex, they pulled over and Roman said, "Take his wallet and throw him into the weeds."

Viktor did as instructed, and as they drove away Roman said, "We'll toss the wallet and the towels into the Hudson.

I've got his phone; we'll toss that too. There are no cameras by the warehouse, so no one could see anything." He pulled out a burner phone and called 911.

Making his voice unrecognizable, Roman said, "There's a man lying in the weeds on the parkway in Bay Ridge by the Beltway. Looks like a bum, but I'm not sure." He hung up.

"We'll dump the burner in the Hudson too. Wipe the prints off everything; there's good access just up the street."

Viktor opened Hyde's wallet and said, "Asshole carries lot of cash. There's few grand in here."

Roman felt his mouth dry as his father pocketed the cash and wiped the prints. Now that it was over, he worried that the intervention between the two men had been the right decision. Hyde was goddamned lucky to be alive, and he sincerely hoped the man wasn't stupid enough to test his father further. But pondering that, Roman wasn't entirely certain, and it made him squirm. *No one could be that fucking stupid, could they?*

As he drove, Roman felt a small chill. His memory flooded as he frantically scoured through their previous encounters, searching for evidence that Hyde had ever displayed any kind of wisdom. It just wasn't there. Lacking complexity and wholly surface, Hyde, in scene after scene, defaulted to his petty base and blustered outrageously idiotic statements, boring everyone in his path as he spewed his bullshit and nauseating self-aggrandizement. He couldn't keep his putrid hole shut. That was Hyde.

Goddamned fucking twat. Hyde might be a walking dead man after all.

Chapter 43

SEVERAL DAYS LATER, Alex Macchi got a call from Clarence Beutz. "So, I don't suppose you heard that Hyde Sutton got mugged, did you?"

Alex feigned surprise and worked his eyebrows up. "Really? That's big. Where did that happen?"

"Interesting, really. He was found in Bay Ridge, right near the warehouse complex."

"Wow, I wonder what he was doing over there?" Alex smiled, thinking of Hyde bloody and lying in the weeds.

"Don't know. Seems he can't remember either. As we both know there's not a lot of cameras around that area. I don't suppose you still have anyone filming from the bird's nest?"

"No. We pulled out after the raid. The operation was shut down, so there was no reason to keep watching."

Clarence said, "That's too bad. It would have been nice to see what happened to him."

"What *did* happen to him? Is he okay?" Alex pumped his fist with excitement, like his team had just scored a home run.

"Yeah. He's home. Has a broken nose, a concussion, and a fairly bad broken wrist," Clarence replied.

"I see."

"So, your brother, the cop—Tony, right? Wasn't he mugged in just about that same area?"

"He was."

"And what kind of injuries did he sustain?"

"He had a concussion and a broken wrist."

Clarence didn't respond right away. "Huh. And they never found out who did that either, is that right?"

"No, but we assumed it was someone from the Timofeyev gang after we got wind about something fishy going down over there."

"Huh. Well just thought I'd ask. I got wind of it through the detectives over there and thought maybe there was a link."

Alex smiled broadly. "I think you should pull on that thread, Clarence. It might just unravel."

"I think I will."

ALEX HUNG UP, satisfied with not only his acting job, but with the elation he felt every time he thought about Hyde's condition. He'd been alerted to the Hyde Sutton attack days earlier when Karla reported the scene from the Hyde home front. He hadn't heard about the Bay Ridge connection, though, and that tidbit was terribly interesting.

It was so interesting, in fact, that the Button Man decided it would be important for his partner at the *New York Post*, Ben Quick, to know about it too. Maybe they could connect the dots, after conducting an investigation, and report it. They were a diligent group.

The Button Man smiled and placed the call.

Chapter 44

A LEX STRETCHED AND PUT his feet up on his office desk as he answered his phone: "Karla, what do you know?"

"It just gets sadder and sadder over here. Yesterday, Hyde was crying in his office while looking at the *Post*... blubbering like a little baby. He seems a little dejected, Alex. If the man weren't such a complete scumbag, I'd actually feel sorry for him."

"Don't bother. I was thinking it might be time to shut it down over there, but we need to get the cameras out and, unfortunately, our charm boy, Owen, is otherwise engaged. That said, I could have him give Bijoux a call and set up a meeting to get you safely in and the hardware out."

"That would work. I can handle it. I'd probably only need fifteen minutes to get it all out. Do you think Owen could possibly find the time to help us?" she asked, sarcastically.

Alex twirled a pencil on his desk. "Yeah, he'll find the time. They're in Hawaii. He's got Carey on a board, and they're working on their tans, but I'll pull him away."

"You sure you want to take it all down? Hyde might be vulnerable right now, but he's still an ass, and he's going to come back."

Alex picked up the pencil, flipped it in the air, and then caught it. "Bacon's got the back door, so we'll leave that unlocked. The rest needs to go. I'll have Owen give Bijoux a call and tell her to expect your call. When you're done, tell Bijoux we think it's time for her to leave the country. Abruptly. Find out what she needs in the way of finances and after she's back in France, we'll follow up on our promise to get her back here and train to be a world-class chef."

"She's a sweet kid, Alex. It's been hard for me to watch the way Hyde treats all of them. Pravdina needs to leave him and get Simone out of reach before he totally corrupts her."

"I'm afraid we've done what we can there, Karla, but I appreciate that you care about them. I think we've all been sucked into the dark world of Hyde Sutton for too long, and it's time to move on. He's not in the clear, by a long shot, with the Feds, the Timofeyevs, or our lawyers for the contractors, for that matter. But I don't want to spend any more of our valuable time analyzing his every word and action.

"He's got a couple of barrels attached to him now, so next time, everyone should see him coming."

OCTOBER

Epilogue

Alex walked into his bedroom and saw Charlotte lying on a chaise longue near the windows overlooking the city and holding their happy two-and-one-half-year-old daughter, Lily. Clothes and toys were scattered on every surface, and Petunia followed him into the room, pulling a suitcase and backpack.

"Mom," she said. "I've finished packing my clothes, but there's no way I'm going to be able to get all the presents for the babies and Aunt Carey and Uncle Owen into my suitcase." Petunia flopped down next to Charlotte and held up a small, framed portrait for them to admire.

"Do you think they'll like it?" she said anxiously. "I haven't met Uncle Owen yet, but Aunt Carey always said she liked my paintings."

"Let me see that," Alex said, carefully stepping over the piles of stuff waiting to be packed. He took the nicely framed wedding gift that his talented daughter had painted and smiled. In the lower left-hand corner Petunia had named the picture "Home." It was a picture of Whispering Cliffs as it's seen when driving up to it. The trees and the colors were vibrant, and the home was formidable—a lovely stalwart against a blue sky.

"It's wonderful, honey," said Alex. "They'll love it."

"Where do you think they'll live? I mean they'll need a place to hang it," she said.

"I don't know, but right now they're home with the rest of them. We can ask them soon enough," said Charlotte.

"I can't wait to meet the babies!" Petunia said, grabbing Lily and swinging her around, delighting both of them.

"Careful there, honey," laughed Charlotte. "Don't trip on anything!"

Petunia kissed her sister on her plump cheek. "I just love the names, too: Velvet and Max. Velvet Sophia Carrows and Maximus Henry Carrows. Twins! They're sooo cute."

"I can't wait to meet them, either. The house is going to be very lively when we get there!" Charlotte grinned from ear to ear as she reached over to grab some items off the floor.

"Your parents will be in their glory," Alex said, handing Charlotte the picture. He found some space to sit on the bed, and Petunia had Lily fly into his arms. "It's only their dream come true."

Charlotte sat on the floor and organized some items in an open suitcase. "It is. I'm so happy for everyone. Angelica sailed through the delivery, and even though they must be exhausted, she sounds strong and happy. Charles doesn't have a clue what's going on," she said laughing. "God, can you just see him running through the house with bottles and nuks and diapers in the middle of the night? One minute he's with the Queen of England, and the next he's got two babies who both need his attention at the same time. It's going to be great to see the show live and in person."

"I'm sure the nanny helps too," Alex said, stretching out on the bed, Lily crawling over him.

"Yes, but only during the day. Angelica wants them to be hands-on parents. Let's face it. I admire that even though it's got Charles way out of his comfort zone. The Renners are making a trip back for the wedding party too. Mom wants to get a family portrait, so I also have some things laid out for that." Charlotte pointed toward another pile.

"We're only going for a week, right?" Alex crinkled his brow as he looked at her sitting among the piles and a large trunk with confusion.

"It'll all fit on the plane. I checked with NetJets, and they've put aside some extra room for us just in case. You know, it might be time for us to look into getting a family plane. We should talk about it when we get there."

"Lily," yelled Petunia, grabbing her hand. "Let's go see if there's anything in your room to bring for the babies!"

Alex and Charlotte watched the girls romp out of the room, and Alex enjoyed the smile of contentment on his wife's face while she tucked long strands of hair behind her ears. Petunia was a lot like her mom. Not just lovely, but strong. They were proud of her decision to stay at the studio with her head held high. She'd told them not to worry so much about her and that she had it handled. While he and Charlotte weren't totally convinced, they instructed Petunia to tell them if Simone, her parents, or her friends ever became a problem. Petunia and Charlotte were close. There'd be no secrets. It was one day at a time. Who knew what the future would bring?

"Are you excited about the trip too, Alex?" Charlotte asked.

He picked up Lily's ever-present blanket, appraising the ordinary treasure. "You know I am. I can't wait to meet the Kai family and see Owen, who I haven't seen since the big event."

"They're happy, so that's all that matters."

"I know; it's just bizarre."

"He and Charles are getting along well. He told me Owen is a natural with the babies *and* with Mom and Dad. He's made a nice first impression on everyone."

Alex laughed. "I'm not at all surprised. Owen could charm a room full of rattlesnakes. It's his special gift."

"You're not saying that my family is a bunch of rattlesnakes, are you?" she sneered playfully.

"Only when they're angry." He tossed Lily's blanket at his beautiful wife and smiled. "Meeting your family, working for them, marrying one of them, and becoming involved in their schemes...well, it's been a real eye-opener. I'm just glad I chose the right team."

"It's time we get back to normal and enjoy what we have: the girls, my growing family, your growing family, our lives together. We're so blessed, Alex."

She came over to the bed, and he pulled her down into his arms. They lay next to each other for a while, and Alex felt peace, grateful, too, for the decisions they'd made to pull the plug on the campaign and for the trafficking operation shutdown. Alex said, "Did you talk to Sarah today?"

"Yes, she's agreed to stay on as the full-time housemother and general wrangler of services. She'll make sure the house is as well cared for as the women are. She met with New Jersey social services, and they know the property is exclusively for the victims of trafficking. The curious neighbors were not anxious to have it become a domestic violence shelter with "children running amok and unsupervised," as one of them put it, but Sarah and social services calmed them. Sadly, between other trafficking operations in New Jersey and New York, the house will have a waiting list. I'm glad we purchased it, Alex, and got involved. I hope it helps some of them put their lives back together."

Alex kissed the top of his wife's lovely head, content that she'd found a way to make peace with their troubles and create something positive. Her passion for helping others and the foundation had grounded them all. "Sue Douglas really helped, too, don't you think?"

Alex was referring to a woman in her thirties named Sue, who was a survivor of human trafficking and shared her story and her strength with the victims. She was an inspiration to everyone who met her, but most importantly to the women who felt as if their world was too dark to recover from.

"Such a spirit. Such a gift. But you know, if she hadn't gone through what she did, she couldn't be there to help the other survivors. It makes you think. It's so sad and twisted that the ones who've suffered have the most to teach."

"And Freya, have you spoken with her?" Alex stroked her arm.

"She'll always have a special place in my heart, and I hope we'll always stay in touch. I can't blame her for not wanting to testify and spend her life in witness protection. My God she's only nineteen years old! And her wonderful parents—she couldn't do that to them either. The DA convinced one of the Russian girls to stay and testify, but that was mostly because she didn't have much of a family back in Russia. She'll be able to start over here, not that she wouldn't trade it all if she didn't have to live through that nightmare. Her testimony should be enough for some convictions."

Alex frowned. "We gave them video evidence. They caught them red-handed. Barring some legal technical catastrophe, I doubt any of them are walking away from this."

"How do we feel about the big fish—Hyde Sutton and Roman and Viktor Timofeyev—not being charged?" Charlotte pulled her head off his chest and looked him in the eye.

"There's always tomorrow. They'll do something, eventually and either the law or some other force will punish them. In the meantime, I'm glad we're moving on. Literally, to Whispering Cliffs, tomorrow."

Charlotte kissed him and then sat up. She reached over and picked up the picture, Petunia's wedding gift for Carey. "Home," she said, smiling. "It all started there."

About the Author

Annabelle Lewis is a pseudonym for the author who lives in Minneapolis with her husband, children, and a wild thug of a dog who sleeps beside her. She has been an avid reader her entire life and when she wasn't busy raising her family, she was writing short stories about them. In addition to fictional work, she publishes a touching, yet oddly scathing blog posted on her website. Get a glimpse behind the curtain and follow her feverish mind! She sincerely appreciates your reviews and support. You can reach Annabelle and follow her blog at:

www.theannabellelewis.com
Annabellelewisauthor@gmail.com
Twitter: @alewisauthor
Facebook: www.facebook/com/Annabellelewisauthor

COMING SOON... Road Trip, Book 7 of the Carrows Family Chronicles

Petunia Carrows Macchi, young daughter of Charlotte and Alex, encourages her family to take a vacation. Unfortunately, she becomes a witness for the prosecution after overhearing a plan to eliminate an innocent young mother in the backwoods of Minnesota lake country.

Made in the USA
Monee, IL
04 March 2022